AT 11:15 HE WOULD CALL SMITH . . .

It was 11:14. At the half-minute, Remo dialed. The phone was answered mid-ring. Remo was surprised at how happy he was to hear even Smitty's voice. But it wasn't Dr. Harold Smith.

"Who am I talking to?" Remo asked.

"New man in the office." The voice had that plastic California quality. "Who are you?"

"I must have a wrong line. I'm looking for Dr. Smith."

"He's on vacation. Can I help you?"

"Where?"

"There's a high-priority restriction on his place frame."

"Who are you?"

"Blake Corbish. I'm the new director here at the sanitarium."

"You've taken over all of Smith's duties?"

"All of them."

"I see," said Remo. He hung up. There was something very wrong. Remo did not know what to do. This would be important to Chiun, but Remo could not decide whether or not to tell him that the House of Sinanju might have to seek a new employer.

An emperor's fall, after all, was a serious thing.

THE DESTROYER SERIES

THE DESTROYER

JUDGMENT DAY

by
Richard Sapir & Warren Murphy

PINNACLE BOOKS • LOS ANGELES

THE DESTROYER: JUDGMENT DAY

Copyright © 1974 by Richard Sapir and Warren Murphy

An original Pinnacle Books edition, published for the
first time anywhere.

ISBN: 0-523-40288-0

First printing, February 1974
Second printing, May 1976
Third printing, February 1977
Fourth printing, April 1978

Printed in the United States of America

PINNACLE BOOKS, INC.
2029 Century Park East
Los Angeles, California 90067

For a store detective, a nude model, a sidewalk peddler, and for the glorious House of Sinanju, P.O. Box 1149, Pittsfield, Massachusetts.

JUDGMENT DAY

CHAPTER ONE

He wanted to know if anyone could hear screams from there. The real estate salesman said he had never thought of the property in those terms. Secluded, yes. Pastoral, yes. Fantastic view, most assuredly. Why didn't Mr. Blake Corbish just look around?

"Yes," agreed Corbish. "A fantastic view . . . but who can see *us* from here?"

Ignoring the plastic happiness of the real estate salesman, Corbish intently examined the cliffside, from the coves down to the lapping blue Pacific outside the small California town of Bolinas. Behind him the lower slopes of Mt. Tamalpais gently rose toward the sky.

He looked left, then right. Almost a mile down the fragile dirt and gravel road he could see a small white cabin. With powerful binoculars a man down there could see all the way up. A man might even be able to hear with the aid of an audio-snooping device. The things that could be done with electronics nowadays were amazing.

But even more amazing was what could be done with

computers. Blake Corbish knew. Why, you could put a whole country on a computer system if you had to. You could program it in such a way that only one man could have access to the final printouts. And if that man was stubbornly selfish with his information, then he should not be allowed to stand in the way of greater good—in the way of Blake Corbish's employer, International Data Corporation, IDC. Not even if he screamed.

"As you see, sir, this house, this property is a rare find for someone who wants seclusion and graciousness."

"Hmmm," said Corbish. He glanced behind him at the sprawling California-style ranch house with the large stone patio that was too open to helicopter view, the wide, glaringly open-view windows that faced the Pacific and the surrounding foothills, the innumerable sliding glass doors that a man could run right through if he were desperate enough or stubborn enough.

"A lovely house, don't you think, Mr. Corbish?"

"Uh, well . . ." Corbish looked down the road again at the white cabin.

"Who owns that?" he asked.

"Oh, you're not interested in that. That's barely insulated, only one improperly working bathroom and the owner wants an unreasonable amount for it."

"Hmmm," mused Corbish. He was in his late thirties, a trim gentleman with clipped brown hair, parted as if with the help of a mechanic's rule, a smooth, slightly tanned face hinting of sailing at the Hamptons and skiing at Vail, a neatly tuned body draped in the elegant simplicity of Brooks Brothers gray, and the strong solid roots of the muted black and orange stripes in his not-too-wide tie. A perfect IDC executive, a model IDC executive, a vice president at thirty-seven. Maybe even the next senior vice president of IDC if there were not thirty others at IDC almost exactly like him on various

10

rungs of the corporate ladder in "the corporation to be in" if you were talking about corporations. And no one talked about anything else in the circles of Blake Corbish.

"Let's see the house," said Corbish in that perfect IDC way that committed nothing and demanded everything.

He endured the flossy enthusiasm of the agent, who described the parquet floors of the bedrooms, the solid stone of the massive fireplace, the new weather control that could create anything indoors from Berkshire autumn to Puerto Rican spring, and, of course, the carpeting. From fireplace right out to patio, indoor-outdoor, and it could take anything from mud to a hurricane and come up pure and clean as the day it was installed. Wall to wall, of course.

"Anything else?" asked Corbish, who did not like the telephones in every room.

"As an executive with IDC, you probably have already noticed the telephones. Well, I must honestly confess, there has been some trouble with telephone service up here. A big storm can put out the phones sometimes. They come up here on one exposed wire. But you can, with your influence, I'm sure, have underground lines put in."

Corbish liked the single exposed line just the way it was. But that was about all he liked. The house was too open, too vulnerable.

"You certainly have made a good presentation," said Corbish. "I'll have to consider it."

"An ideal property like this is sure to move quickly."

"I imagine it is," said Corbish. He moved to the door. There were several other properties he would check out today.

"And there's the deep basement. I don't imagine you'd

11

be interested in that. One basement is pretty much like another."

Deep basement.

"Since I'm already here, I might as well take a look," said Corbish.

"I feel I should explain," said the real estate agent. "You can use it for storage or you can panel it, fix it up. It doesn't look too pretty now. You see, the builder at the time was caught up in the bomb shelter craze when everyone was afraid of atomic war. It's not really a basement. It's a lead-lined deep hole in the ground with special air filtering ducts and, well, it's sort of spooky. We could have it done over as a basement playroom before you'd even be ready to move in."

Blake Corbish examined the deep basement once and told the real estate agent he not only didn't mind the basement, he wanted the keys to the house right away.

"Then you wish to buy?"

"Definitely. And I want that little white cabin down the road too."

"The banks here don't like to give mortgages on second homes," said the real estate agent.

"IDC doesn't need mortgages," said Corbish. "I want the sale consummated within twenty-four hours."

"That white cabin really isn't worth the price, if I may say so, sir."

"IDC wants it."

The real estate agent grinned, flush-faced.

"Well, anything IDC wants, IDC gets."

"We use positive corporate policy, yes," said Corbish.

"I read about you in Forbes, I believe, Mr. Corbish. You are one of the youngest vice presidents at IDC."

"There are thirty vice presidents at IDC," said Corbish coldly.

"You're exceptional, according to what I read."

"We're all exceptional."

"Then how do they decide who becomes president?"

"Whoever makes the strongest contributions becomes president. We know, down to the very digit."

"Yes," the salesman agreed. "I've heard that mentioned about IDC, that your advanced computer research puts you a generation ahead of everyone else in the field."

"Positive corporate approach," said Corbish coldly. He endured the real estate salesman's never-ending sales talk all the way back into San Francisco, thirty miles to the south.

Corbish would not have had a man like that in *his* organization. He didn't know his job. A good salesman stops selling when he has made the sale. More often than not, he can lose an already-made sale by offering too much information. One should only give a prospect enough information to make the sale and no more.

Information was the true base of power of IDC. Other companies made computers. Other companies designed computer programs. Only IDC had the whole package, the designing, the pure science, the construction and the operation. Competitors were into computers; IDC was into information.

But no corporation could thrive with only one product, and as IDC moved farther into acquisitions of lumber, oil, coal, aluminum, transistors and real estate—not just the purchase of a little Pacific coastline house, but vast tracts of undeveloped land—the executive teams began to realize that they needed even more information. There was a scarcity of knowledge about what went on in those other fields.

Like taxes, for instance. With computers, one could predict what price the competition would charge, right to the penny. But one could not predict what the politicians would decide to spend, unless of course one

13

owned the local politicians. Owning them was much more easy if you could learn their secrets. Money could not *always* buy a politician but information could.

In America, on the shores of Long Island Sound, there was a mother lode of such information, beyond IDC's wildest projections. Information on who paid what taxes, which people took what payoffs, where narcotics entered the country, who sold what to whom and when, even the effect of weather on commodities futures was calculated. The works. And no one at this place called Folcroft Sanitarium, on the shores of Long Island Sound, seemed to be using that information to its fullest advantage. It seemed a crime against nature that IDC did not have access to it. Blake Corbish intended to amend that crime.

At the San Francisco Airport, Blake Corbish prepared the flight plan of his Lear jet to Westchester Airport, a few scant miles from Rye, New York. He was told there would be some sticky weather over Colorado. Corbish said he would fly above it.

The man at the control tower seemed impressed by Corbish's knowledge of aeronautics. So impressed that he asked questions about Corbish's training, very nicely, very politely.

Corbish was polite in return. The man at the control tower might be one of the thousands of people who unknowingly fed information into those computers at Folcroft. If that were so, then this man would be working for IDC soon—also without knowing it.

Only a genius could have set up the computers at Folcroft so that only one man had the information at his terminal. Only one man, so far as Corbish knew now, understood how it worked. The beauty of the entire organizational set up was that the people who worked in it had at best only a fragmentary idea of what they

14

were doing. Most thought they worked for private companies; the shrewder ones suspected they were informants for the FBI, but none knew that he was really working to help fill up the computer data banks at Folcroft. So brilliantly was this organization set up, that big firms, even IDC, supplied it with workers, unawares.

Only one thing puzzled Corbish and that was the reason for this organization, whose code name was CURE. No one appeared to profit from it. It was not a military operation, even though it had some military approaches to matters. A military operation worked against armies and governments; CURE seemed simultaneously to work for some American citizens and work against some American citizens.

Corbish thought about this as his Lear jet climbed over the weather in Colorado. He would have all the answers within two days. It was ironic that the computers at Folcroft had told him he would have the information in two days. That too was on one of the readouts he had waylaid. An extensive study of torture. It told him what he had always suspected in his years as a special forces captain before joining IDC: any man will tell you anything if you torture him properly. No special drugs, no esoteric brainwashing. If you could convince a man that he could stop the pain you inflicted on him by what he told you, and that he could stop the pain forever if he told you what you wanted, he would tell. The human animal was like that. Any man could be broken within forty-eight hours. Stories about people resisting torture were, by and large, nonsense. Only when the interrogator failed to connect pain with information did people remain mum. It was not moral weakness that made people talk, it was the very essence of human nature itself. Stop pain and survive. It was that simple.

15

Corbish crossed the plains states and could not help thinking of the IDC offices there, especially in Kansas City. Why, those people at CURE were even plugged into a payroll computer there used by a professional sports complex.

The weather would be good over Westchester. Corbish checked that on his radio. He also ordered refueling for the New York stop.

"I want the jet checked out for another cross country. Back to San Francisco in the morning."

"That's a lot of flying."

"I'm a man on the move," said Corbish. "Over and out."

Funny that the control tower should say "That's a lot of flying." The chairman of the board had used that phrase. It was a drizzly day in Mamaroneck, New York, when the chairman of the board had asked for a special meeting. Corbish had been vice president in charge of international relations, which was six stepping stones to senior vice president in charge of policy planning, which was the final stepping stone to the presidency. The president–chairman of the board was not smiling when Corbish entered. He was alone, which was unusual for an IDC executive whose whole training had been geared to working in committees. Corbish could not remember ever having met another high-ranking executive alone, not even on a golf course.

The president and chairman of the board also had that clean-cut, bright, aggressive and reliable sort of look, with twenty-five years added to it in the form of facial lines and graying hair.

"Sit down," he said. "This meeting will take no more than five minutes. You will not remember this meeting, nor will I. We shall never meet alone again, nor will you ever discuss this with me again. When you have successfully finished your assignment, you will tell me 'done'

16

and begin showing me the effects of what you have achieved. Within a week after that date, you will rise to senior vice president in charge of policy planning. Do you follow me?"

"I follow you, T.L., but I don't understand you."

"Near here—funny that it is near here—is a sanitarium. Folcroft Sanitarium. It has the 385, 971 and the 842 computer systems."

"The 842 is part of a new generation of computers that isn't supposed to be on the market for two years."

"Correct. They own it."

"But we only lease our computers. We never sell them."

"They own it and they have some of our top-flight research people working on it, a concentration of talent we never allow out of IDC."

"How could that happen?"

"Do you remember in one of your early training sessions you learned that you could, if you had enough money and talent, put an entire country, its main sources of power, all on a computer system?"

"Yes."

"Folcroft Sanitarium in Rye, New York, has done it. You will be the next senior vice president in charge of policy planning because you are the only vice president we have with special forces training and I wouldn't give this to anyone else. This should give you an inkling of where we wish you to set your parameters on this assignment."

"What I understand, T.L., is that there are none. I should stop at nothing."

"I didn't hear that, Corbish."

"What will happen if I fail?"

"Then we will have to commit a broad-scale executive thrust in that direction."

17

"Wouldn't IDC be wiser to just write me off if I fail and continue business as usual?"

"These people at Folcroft, I believe, don't just forget about people, corporations or organizations that threaten them. They would come after us, I believe."

"Then, T.L., I must ask you one more question. Why not leave them alone if the risk of failure is so great? There is a point of diminishing returns. I'm afraid my input has got to weigh on the side of another look-see in depth. IDC comes ahead of my personal advancement from my view strata, T.L."

And this was the first time Blake Corbish, vice president, ever saw in T.L. Broon emotion other than responsible optimism or cautious concern. It was anger. A blood-flushing, red-rising anger that boiled from T.L. Broon's corporate soul.

"They have undermined the profit structure of IDC," he said, his voice quivering with rage. "Undermined the very profit structure of IDC, by hijacking our computer systems, by competing with us in the field of total information. If another corporation thought of doing this, we would crush it. If a politician thought of doing this, we would defeat him. If a banker tried it, we would bankrupt him. Do you understand? The two of us cannot exist together."

"Can do, sir," said Corbish in a phrase reminiscent of his brief Army career when everyone was talking about the problems of Vietnam and all the younger military men were saying "can do." It was the way captains became majors and majors became colonels. It was the way a vice president could become senior vice president in charge of policy planning before he was forty.

"You've got a lot of flying to do, Blake. Get to it," T.L. had said.

There were a couple of problems with Folcroft, but

18

Corbish being a top-flight operations man, made sure his approach was secure and thorough. He didn't rush into Folcroft. Instead he sent people to repair computers, to examine bills, to attempt to sell new software and hardware, keeping himself out of the picture to see what Folcroft's corporate response would be.

Two programmers Corbish never saw again; a third was found with his chest crushed to jelly on a Long Island beach. The coroner had sent detectives to look for some huge hydraulic machine—he explained that only a machine like that could have performed such a body-splashing killing. But it was obvious the programmer had been killed on the beach and any machine capable of that sort of force would have left marks.

IDC dutifully paid death benefits to the families—IDC always took care of its own—and with the final death, Corbish had his point of operations bracketed. He focused his attention on a rather prim, middle-aged man, with a mind so addled he even refused a top executive position with IDC.

Dr. Harold Smith, director of Folcroft Sanitarium, was the man with the office that had the only computer terminal that took all the hookups from all the computers and unscrambled them. It was a brilliant system, Corbish thought. But the man running it was too stubborn. Perhaps that was a function of late middle age, another reason why IDC retired its executives before they became doddering, senile, and worst of all, stubborn.

There was no room in the corporate world for stubbornness. That was old-fashioned, outmoded, obsolete as the abacus. People became obsolete also. Too bad for Dr. Smith.

Corbish's landing at Westchester Airport was, as usual, perfect. He was a careful, impeccable flyer who, though

19

he entertained no fear—not even in the most hazardous storms—never indulged in unnecessary risks. There were old pilots and bold pilots, he knew, but never any old bold pilots.

He supervised the refueling, discussed checking out the craft with one of the few mechanics he trusted, then drove away in his wife's station wagon which he had parked there two days before. He thought of phoning her to say hello, but decided against it. He did not want to waste the time. It would not hurt to be a few minutes early for his evening meeting with Dr. Smith. Better a few minutes early than a second late.

Corbish drove through the high gates of Folcroft with the rising brick walls that discreetly hid everything, and parked his station wagon alongside the administration building in the back. Only one light was on. It came from Smith's office with the one-way glass that emitted just a faint glimmer of light at night, but obscured any shapes. Within forty-eight hours, according to the best research on the subject, Corbish would see all he wanted about Folcroft. He would see everything with utmost clarity.

By happenstance, Corbish glanced into the clean dark night at the awesome array of stars whose distance and magnitude had remained mysterious before the advent of the computer. Seeing the eternity of space, Corbish, for reasons he did not know, thought of a perplexing readout from Folcroft. It had referred to The Destroyer, some kind of navy ship obviously, and to a little village in North Korea called Sinanju.

CHAPTER TWO

His name was Remo and he was making a polite visit to a Detroit suburb, a gracious large-lawned sprawling house in Grosse Pointe, miles from the inner city where people injected death into their arms or sniffed it or sold it in "protected" houses.

Those who used the product that provided the income that enabled this lawn to get a daily manicure, the house to receive daily cleaning by two maids, the swimming pool to remain heated and functioning—all winter—were not allowed in this neighborhood. If they were seen walking the streets after dark, policemen asked them what they were doing. Unless they could name a house where they were going to tend bar, make beds, or take out garbage, they were whisked away. They were very easy to spot in this neighborhood because black faces stood out very well.

Remo's face did not stand out. He had high cheekbones and dark eyes that seemed to go on for eternity and the paleness of a just lost tan. He was about six feet tall and, except for his large wrists, appeared almost lean. He rang the doorbell of the Jordan home, a name which had once been Giordano when Angelo Giordano was running numbers in downtown Detroit, before he had found the awesome profitability of bulk-supplying black pushers with the white powder that continued its fine sales despite a lack of advertising and the marketing handicaps, like fifteen years to life.

Arnold Jordan had so many broken links between himself and the final sale, that it was very unlikely that he would personally face these handicaps. That was for the little men.

A maid answered the door.

"Good evening," said Remo. "I'm from the Grosse Pointe Homeowners' League and I would like to talk with Mr. Jordan."

"Is Mr. Jordan expecting you?"

"No," said Remo.

"If you would wait here, I'll see if Mr. Jordan is at home."

"Thank you," said Remo. He began to whistle somewhat nervously while he waited for a reply. He had an unusually busy schedule for the evening. Upstairs—where his orders came from—had become highly unreasonable recently, almost bordering on the worst of all possible sins, incompetence. It was this IDC thing. It had to be the IDC thing, although Remo had not even been formally notified that there was such a thing as an IDC thing. He had just been given the names and general whereabouts of three computer programmers. Disposing of the last one on a Long Island beach had taken fifteen seconds. Remo spent the first fourteen of them laughing as the man had assumed some sort of silly Kung Fu stance, which was fine for a martial arts school, but which left the chest as open as the ocean.

Remo did not know the name of the stance, because

as the Master of Sinanju—Remo's trainer—had explained, one should not waste precious time cataloguing someone else's foolishness. Sinanju, unlike the known variations of the martial arts, was not an art but a working tool. Less and less could Remo fathom how people would want to make games out of daily work, even devoting leisure hours to it. But then there were even lawyers who mowed lawns for relaxation.

The maid, in starched white apron, returned with apologies that Mr. Jordan was unavailable.

"It will just take a minute. I'm really in a rush," said Remo, gliding around the maid who could have sworn she had a hand out there to stop him. She watched the visitor seem to slip through it as she stood there, hand upraised in empty air.

Arnold Jordan was having dinner with his family. He was poised with a forkful of blueberry pie when Remo entered the somewhat overfurnished dining room.

"I'm awfully sorry to bother you," said Remo. "This will only take a minute. Finish your pie. Go ahead. Don't let me bother you."

Jordan, a massive man with the strong rocklike face of a Roman legionnaire but the styled dry hair of a TV announcer, put down his fork.

"Go ahead, finish it," said Remo. "You like blueberry pie?"

"May I ask who you are?"

"Grosse Pointe Homeowners' League. It will only take a minute. I really don't have more than a minute for you anyhow."

"You can phone my secretary in the morning. I am eating now."

"I said, finish it."

Arnold Jordan wiped his mouth with the fine white linen napkin, excused himself from the table, receiving scarcely a nod of recognition from his wife and children.

"I will give you a minute," said Jordan heavily. "But I think I should warn you that you are not doing yourself any good by interrupting my supper."

Remo merely nodded. He did not have time for polite chitchat. Jordan led Remo into a book-lined den.

"All right. What's your name? What are you here for? What's your employer's name? I told you, you didn't do yourself any good by interrupting my supper. I want his name and phone number."

"His name's Smith, but don't worry about making any phone calls. That's not why I'm here. You see, you've just connected with a massive shipment, and it's so big I was sent to dispose of it." Remo muttered under his breath, "No one bothered to think that I can't be two places at one time or there are so many hours in the day. No, just go to Jordan's house, find out where it is, then do the normal thirty-five hours work in one night. And we're supposed to be efficient."

"I beg your pardon," said Jordan.

"C'mon. I don't have all night," said Remo.

"That's right," said Jordan. "That's very right. You don't have all night at all. Now why don't you do yourself a very big favor and leave."

"I take it that's one of your subtle threats."

Jordan shrugged his shoulders. He estimated that he could crack this man in two if he had to, but why should he have to. He merely had to phone the police and have the man arrested for trespassing. Then when the man was released in his own recognizance, he would prove that the courts were too lenient by just disappearing. Perhaps in Lake Michigan.

Jordan's self assurance was somewhat shaken by a searing, biting pain in his right shoulder. It felt like a hot iron. His mouth opened to scream but there was no

24

sound. Just the pain and his visitor's forefinger and thumb where the pain was. Jordan could neither move nor speak.

He sat at his desk, like a frog that had just had its stomach rubbed, helpless.

"All right," said the visitor. "This is pain."

The shoulder felt as if hot needles pricked the socket. But the visitor's fingers hardly moved.

"This is an absence of pain."

Jordan felt a relief so blessed he almost cried.

"You can have an absence of pain, or this."

The hot needles again.

"This goes when I find out where the heroin shipment is."

Jordan tried to speak but he had no voice.

"I don't hear you."

Jordan tried to yell but he couldn't.

"You've got to speak up."

Didn't this man realize that he couldn't speak? He was a crazy and the shoulder felt as if it were coming out of the socket and Jordan would say anything, tell anything, if only his voice would cooperate. He felt the pain shift to his chest and suddenly his vocal cords were free but he could hardly breathe.

Hoarsely he mentioned a "protected" house downtown. But the crazy visitor wouldn't believe him, just kept saying that it wasn't true.

"My god, I swear it's true. Fifty-five kilos. I swear it. My god, please believe me, it's true. Please. The heroin's behind a wooden panel that secures the front door. Believe me."

"I do," said the visitor. And then the pain was magnificiently, gloriously, joyously gone and a sudden night descended on Angelo Giordano, alias Arnold Jordan, who encountered the ultimate marketing difficulty that can result from merchandising heroin.

Remo put the body in a lounging chair, closed Jordan's eyes, and left the room, jamming the lock to give himself twenty to thirty minutes. He expressed regrets to the Jordan family that he could not stay for dessert, and told Mrs. Jordan her husband was busy working on a decomposition and should not be disturbed.

"Composition, you mean," said Mrs. Jordan.

Remo did not have time to explain. Once again, Smitty had overloaded a work night, probably because of those computers. Remo had no faith in computers. He had faith in only one thing now and that was a person: an elderly wisp of an Oriental who could so often make Remo's life unpleasant. It was strange to have lost his faith in almost everything else in the last decade, but that might be because, as Chiun, the Master of Sinanju, had told him, his very essence was changing. Dr. Smith, on the other hand, had ascribed the change to a massive transformation of the nervous system not yet understood in the west.

Whatever it was, he could not get himself to the inner city of Detroit and back out to the airport in less than an hour. He would have to risk missing the fifty-five kilos or risk missing the fourth IDC man that Smith had instructed him to eliminate. Remo noticed there was an absence of pay phones in Grosse Pointe. He had to walk three miles before he found a cab, and it was another twelve minutes before they reached a phone booth.

A line was to have been kept open for him all evening. It would be an insecure line, but what it lacked in privacy it made up for in availability. No one could secure a random pay phone.

The booth smelled more like a urinal than a phone booth. Remo dialed the 800 area code number. That meant that a dime from anywhere could reach it. It rang four times. Remo hung up and dialed again. With the phone system working the way it was, it was possible to get a wrong number. He dialed again. Again it rang and Remo counted to five rings.

He hung up and dialed "O."

"Operator, there's some trouble with the lines. I must be getting a wrong number. It just rings."

Remo gave her the number with the 800 area code.

"It's ringing, sir," said the operator.

"It's got to be answered," Remo said.

"I'm sorry, sir. Would you like me to try it again?"

"Yes, thank you."

Again the number rang and no one answered.

"It's ringing, sir."

"I fucking hear you," said Remo. He threw the receiver across the street and the metal-wrapped line popped like a dried-out rubber band.

The cab driver waiting at the curb saw this and said that he had suddenly gotten an emergency phone call. Since he had to leave so abruptly there would be no charge.

Remo wouldn't hear of it. He gave the driver the address of the house which probably still had the fifty-five kilos. The heroin could fly at the first warning and once it was broken down into nickel packs, it could never be destroyed. Remo would just have to hope that the IDC programmer would wait. Besides, Dr. Smith must be miscalculating if Remo had to make so many hits in the IDC thing, whatever it was. A well-thought-out operation should have only one elimination in it, two at the most.

Remo got into the cab, but the driver stood by the door.

"That house you're talking about, buddy, is in a black neighborhood."

"That's nice," said Remo.

Remo's mind wandered. Was it possible that the phone had rung in Smith's office in Folcroft and no one was there to answer it? No. If Dr. Harold Smith said he would be at a certain place at a certain time, Dr. Harold Smith was at that place at that time with disgusting regularity.

Maybe Smitty had had a heart attack and died? Probably not. Remo hadn't had any good luck all evening. Why start now? The cab still wasn't moving. The driver stood by the door.

"C'mon, c'mon," said Remo.

"I ain't driving to a black neighborhood at this hour of night."

"I see your point," Remo said. "But I've got to get there and you're the only way."

"No way, mister."

Remo felt in his pocket for some bills. He took out five of them. Three were tens and two were twenties.

"What good's money to a corpse?" asked the driver.

Remo did a very funny thing with the bulletproof shield which was supposed to separate driver from passenger. Applying pressure to the weak bolt points, he snapped it off. This impressed the driver, who suddenly thought a person should be driven anywhere if he had the fare. Remo insisted the driver take the money and even some extra for the shield. The driver noted how glad he was that his passenger tended to vent most of his hostility on property, not people.

A "protected" house is a relatively new innovation of the heroin trade. Instead of sending pushers out into the warring streets, where they can be ripped off by junkies, the junkies go to these houses to get a fix on the premises or to take out if they desire.

The houses are well supplied with weapons and even with what is called a hot needle—a syringe containing poison—should a buyer be suspected of being a narco cop. They have many fine locks, very thick doors and barred windows. In this respect they are not unlike the liquor stores in the same general neighborhoods.

For the fifty-five kilos, special precautions were taken. No small time customers were allowed; extra men with guns were placed inside the window openings. The front door was reinforced by plywood panels and two-by-fours that moved away so customers could be admitted. All the windows were nailed shut and the basement doors boarded and nailed.

It was the perfect defense. Against just about anything but a penny book of matches and a gallon of gasoline.

As Remo watched the front of the house flame up to become a funeral pyre for its inhabitants and an incinerator for the fifty-five kilos hidden inside the front door, he thought he heard the cab driver crying. But when he asked him, the driver said he was not crying. He was happy. He was happy because he loved his passenger with all his heart and soul.

"Lucky we're dealing with a slum neighborhood; although sometimes you get some good structures here that won't burn," said Remo.

Boy, did the cab driver think his passenger was right. Absolutely. Always thought that himself. Yes, sir. Was the passenger happy? Because the only thing the driver wanted was to keep his passenger happy. To the airport? Absolutely, sir.

At the airport, Remo discovered the IDC programmer was still waiting. Remo apologized for being late, said he would talk to the man in the men's lavatory. Remo left him in a pay toilet to be discovered only when the janitors realized the same still legs had been in the booth too long for even the most severe constipation.

"Rush, rush," muttered Remo as he quickly left the airport in another cab. If things had been properly assigned, he would not have had to run from an assignment so carelessly.

But strange things were coming from upstairs and Remo did not want to think about what they might mean. For as much as he often hated the parsimonious, bitter-faced, unredeemed-by-any-human-warmth Dr. Harold Smith, he did not want to have to exercise the final option against him.

CHAPTER THREE

The report was wrong. The old man had not broken in forty-eight hours. Oh, it looked like it, but all Corbish got was a very clever cover story about a gigantic undercover operation. A waste of precious time.

Why hadn't the report on interrogation told how hard it was to torture someone? Corbish felt the perspiration drip down the small of his back and the stethoscope was wet to his touch as he placed it over the white-haired chest and listened to the heartbeat. Good. The heartbeat was still good. Did this old fool wish to die? Corbish checked his watch again. He was well into the second day. The lead-lined cellar of the house near Bolinas had suffered a breakdown in one of the air ducts, so now it was not only incredibly hot but oxygen was getting scant. He removed the stethoscope from the chest and saw that the chest was now swelling in massive red welts where he had placed the electrodes. He had thought torture would be so easy, and now he realized he was outside the proper time projection for reasonable project success. Everything had worked so well until he had strapped Dr. Smith onto the table of the lead-lined room.

The meeting at Folcroft three days ago had gone perfectly. Corbish had set himself up as an informer who wished not to be seen lest he lose his job at IDC. Dr. Smith had gone for the story, agreeing to the late night meeting. Corbish had limited his externally observable acts to the time between his first contact with Smith, pretending to be an informer, and the night meeting. Like the Japanese beginning peace meetings with America before its fleet set off for Pearl Harbor to find the American navy berthed fat and lazy that sleepy Sunday morning.

Smith had greeted him somewhat cautiously that night, but not cautiously enough. He had kept the desk between them, and Corbish guessed that the office had a scanner at the door that would not have allowed him to bring in a weapon. At least, not a metal weapon. Thus, Smith considered himself safe.

"I suppose you're wondering why I, as a vice president of IDC, want to leave my job and work for you?" said Corbish.

"It had crossed my mind," said Smith, "especially since this is a social research center."

"Well, I know it isn't," Corbish said. He sat across the desk, more than an arm's length away from Smith. All the trinkets on the desk that could be used as weapons, the sharp-edged calendar, the heavy telephone, the pen set, were all on Smith's side of the desk. Even the picture of his wife, an incredibly unattractive woman, was on Smith's side instead of the visitor's, where it would ordinarily be placed so that Smith could see it better.

"You know Folcroft isn't a social research institute?" said Smith smiling. "Well, I know it isn't also. It's a country club for scientists, but I hope to change that."

"It's not that either," said Corbish, "and before I get into that I'd like to explain why I want to join."

Dr. Smith looked puzzled. Perfect acting, thought Corbish.

"Well, you're already here," said Smith. "I think you might be confusing us with someone else. But go ahead. I don't know what I can do for you though."

"I know what I can do for you, sir, and I think you'll agree with me when I outline these five points about what the International Data Corporation is doing."

Corbish asked for a piece of paper. Smith reached into the desk drawer and handed him a sheet of onionskin. Corbish took a small ballpoint pen out of his pocket. It was light blue with the IDC markings in white.

"Do you have something thicker? This paper rips if you write on it."

"Sanitarium stationery?" said Smith. "But frankly I'm not sure I want you writing crazy things on our letterhead. We're heavily government funded and any bad publicity . . ."

"I'll return the stationery to you. After all, it is for your eyes only."

Dr. Smith had nodded, shrugged, made a comment about not knowing what was going on. Before he could slide the sheet of paper across the desk, Corbish was up, politely reaching for it.

"Thank you," he said and jammed the point of the pen into Smith's hand, drawing blood. For a middle-aged man, Smith moved quickly, which was just fine with Corbish. A man moving quickly made his heart move more quickly, and that moved the blood more quickly, and before Smith could reach for something underneath his desk, the blood had carried the drug through his system, and he collapsed in his chair.

It was then that Corbish noticed he had jammed the

pen so deep into Smith's right hand that it was bloody up to the I in the IDC logo. Corbish had been more nervous that he had thought.

From his inside jacket pocket he took what appeared to be a portable raincoat, except that it was thinner and stronger and more opaque. When he unfolded it he had a large plastic bag. Into this bag he pushed the fallen Smith, careful to keep his head near the two small holes in the top. He inserted two tubes that looked like tiny pill bottles and wedged them tight into Smith's cheeks between teeth and gums. The body would have air.

On the way to his car, his theory about CURE proved correct. In an effort to maintain its cover as a harmless research center, there were no guards in the administration building. In an effort to maintain secrecy, CURE had no more protection and security than any other social sanitarium. A part-time guard was at the gate; he was probably a retired policeman. Corbish woke him up driving through. IDC would not keep a person like that. He did not even ask about the plastic bag in the backseat.

Corbish would have to find out why CURE was able to function without guards or gates or questions to visitors, he thought. The flight back to the West Coast was perfect, although he had to fly through some weather, unable to risk putting an oxygen mask on the unconscious Smith.

The car he had rented the day before was waiting at the San Francisco Airport. Even the drive up the twisting Route 1 and then along the mountain path to his special home seemed smooth. As he passed the white cabin on his way up, he saw that it was already boarded up. Excellent. He had only asked that it be vacated, then boarded up later. What was the cover story he had used with the real estate man? He wanted seclusion from the pressure of business, that was it. Naturally, the salesman believed he had purchased the house as an executive love nest. That was just what Corbish wanted. The best cover stories were those where you let someone believe he had discovered something you wanted hidden, something embarrassing.

Corbish was an expert at getting through cover stories, but had never seen a person who had so many layers to one as Smith.

He had put Dr. Smith on the floor of the deep lead-lined cellar, then gotten a kitchen table from upstairs. The house had come furnished. He tied the hands with leather straps he had fashioned at home from old belts. He had picked up a stethoscope in a pawnshop.

He had strapped Smith down and waited for him to revive. The pen had gone so deep that it was well into the next day before the old man opened his eyes. When he did so, Corbish first offered the proposition. Tell him about CURE's operation and there would be no pain. Smith played dumb, then Corbish began with the homemade electrodes he had fashioned. The old man jumped. Corbish worked all over Smith's body and then came the first cover story. It was a foreign operation.

That story went after the first day. And then Smith was silent until forty-eight hours into the operation when, with Corbish himself suffering from lack of sleep, Dr. Harold Smith told him a wild story about an organization set up by the United States government more than ten years before.

When the organization had been set up, the country had a choice between becoming a police state or a mass of chaos that would inevitably end in a dictatorship of the right or the left. The Constitution had been breaking down. Its individual freedoms enabled criminals to function freely. What the President had wanted was an organization outside the law, to make the law work. The government could not acknowledge its existence because that would be acknowledging that the Constitution did not work. Only three men would know about its operation. The President, Smith, and—this was where the story became wild—one other man, the enforcement arm of the agency.

"One man? For the entire country?" Corbish had repeated as he set the electrodes on Smith's groin. The area was already swollen and Smith did not scream. Corbish tested the circuit and it was functioning. It was then that Corbish realized that the old man had passed out.

Now it was well into the third day and Corbish began again, this time with lighted cigarettes. The danger of burning was that it could become infected. Burns were very susceptible to this and he did not wish to make this man a corpse before the successful conclusion of his project. IDC had not become IDC by promoting failures to senior vice president in charge of policy planning.

The old man began whimpering, then groaning. He came to with a scream. Corbish put some water on his lips.

"Now I'm a reasonable man. I want you to be a reasonable man. We deal in reason. Right?"

"Yes," said Smith in a faint whisper. Corbish could see the veins in his head throb.

"I didn't hear you," said Corbish and put his cigarette out on Smith's right leg. The flesh sizzled, and the pulpy skin extinguished the ember.

"Yes, yes," screamed Smith.

"All right. Now reasonably explain to me how this one man can act as your enforcement arm?"

"Sinanju. The Master of Sinanju."

"He is the Master of Sinanju?"

"No. He is the only white man who knows the secrets."

"I see. And with this Sinanju, this white man can do anything?"

"Practically. His nervous system isn't quite human anymore."

"Don't people tend to recognize him? I mean, he must be a very busy man."

"From time to time, Remo has had plastic surgery."

"Remo. I see. And wouldn't his mother recognize him?"

"He's an orphan."

"Wouldn't his friends recognize him?"

"He doesn't have any. They think he died in an electric chair. No prints either."

"Well, that's a lovely way to eradicate identity. Now this Sinanju, tell me about it. It is karate, judo, kung fu?"

"No. They are only beams, but not the light."

"Very poetic. Will you tell me how it works?"

"I don't know. I don't know. I don't know," said Smith and tears formed in his eyes because he did not know and could not give an answer and whenever he did not given an answer there was the pain again.

"Now, now," said Corbish gently. "Let's get to the real truth and there will be no more pain."

Smith became convulsed with sobbing. Corbish wiped the perspiration from his own brow.

"All right," he said. "Let's try the computers. I know computers and I have some questions for you."

"It's the truth," said Smith. "It's the truth."

"All right, all right," said Corbish as if he were talking to a baby.

And then began the line of questioning about information sources, payrolls, the absence of project knowledge by its personnel and surprisingly, all these things made sense. Corbish saw how Smith could have a portion of the IDC payroll on his staff without them knowing of

37

it, and how he could get the new generation of computers even before IDC's most prized customers.

He saw how telephone code words would trigger operations, how government research subsidies could be turned into operating funds for any purpose, and how, with correct programming and brilliant use of personnel, one success could lead to another, so that the person at top could obtain incredible information, fantastic leverage, the ability to get anybody to do anything. Right up to the White House.

The programming, the concepts, the execution of it all, made it seem far away from this whimpering shell of a man who was supposed to have planned it.

For the first time in three days, Corbish left the room. He checked one of the phone codes, a minor thing, that hooked up into Dewline weather forecasts, the early warning device that protected America's air space over Alaska and Canada. Surprisingly, he got a forecast that was followed by weather patterns over Russia, China and France, the only other three nations that had nuclear weapons.

Corbish cupped his face in his hands while he thought. He felt the heavy growth of beard. Suddenly he realized how refreshing the afternoon sun was over Bolinas.

He thought of one more question for Smith. Why, if he had all this power at his fingertips, didn't he take over the government? Or even IDC, for that matter?

But when he returned to the deep cellar, Smith was unconscious. Corbish unshackled the old man, put some water to his lips, but he did not move. He hoisted him to a corner, opened some cans of food and left the stuffy, fetid room. Since the shelter only locked from the inside, Corbish wedged an iron bar through the outside handle of the door. If Smith lived, there might be more questions.

Corbish shaved himself, washed, and made a phone call. It was to T. L. Broon. He got his secretary.

"Tell T. L. that Blake Corbish called. Just tell him 'done.' Thank you," said Corbish, and he went outside the house and ripped out the telephone wire.

He took a helicopter from the Marin County Airport to San Francisco, where he boarded a superjet liner and had his first good meal at a New York restaurant. He hired a chauffeur then to take him to Folcroft sanitarium, which was just beginning a bustling ordinary Tuesday morning—with one exception.

The difference was that usually only Dr. Smith knew the real purposes of Folcroft Sanitarium. But now, a different man knew. Blake Corbish went to Smith's office. The secretary told him Dr. Smith was not in this morning and she did not have an appointment for a Mr. Corbish.

"In the back of your top left drawer is an envelope with instructions for you," said Corbish. Smith had given him the procedure for the change of CURE's directors, but it had been given out when Smith was delirious and Corbish was not really sure it was accurate. Still, if it should fail, he had a secondary plan that involved access to the computer complex.

But it wasn't necessary. He felt a pleasant sense of assured success when indeed there was an envelope in the back of the top left drawer. The envelope was sealed with wax. It had dust on it.

"You know, when I first came here, I wondered what was in this envelope. And Dr. Smith said that one day I would be told to open it. Well, at first I was curious, but then I forgot about it. So many peculiar ways he has."

Inside the envelope was a typewritten sheet; Corbish could tell that it had been written with one of the earliest IDC typewriters from the old typeface and the heavy impression.

The secretary pursed her lips.

"I see," she said. "Well, let's see. There's one of four things I'm supposed to ask you to do. I'll give you a choice. Get me my own tax return or my father's for any year I name, or the weather of China, France, and Russia, or . . ."

Corbish used the secretary's phone for the weather. He did not even let her finish the list. He put the receiver to her ear, she nodded, and he hung up.

"Well, I hope you'll enjoy your stay at Folcroft, sir. Is Dr. Smith all right?"

Corbish could see the honest concern in her face. She might make a good secretary.

"He's fine."

"Good. I'm so glad. When he didn't show up for three days, I was worried, but his wife didn't even seem to bat an eye. Well, I'll tell you, three days for Dr. Smith to be out of this office is very unusual. Very unusual. But then, he has his own way of doing things. A strange man, if you know what I mean, but a fine man. A decent man. A good man."

As Corbish entered his new office with the one-way mirrors that looked out to the Long Island Sound, he made a note to himself that he would have to get rid of this talky old biddy. Loyalty was one thing. Yakety yak was another. An IDC subsidiary, such as Folcroft had just become, did not allow yakety yak.

40

CHAPTER FOUR

A match? Why didn't he use a bomb? A tornado? A flood? An earthquake?

Why hadn't Remo used a car or an electric toaster or a plastic neon-coated sign?

"But Little Father," complained Remo, "there is no such thing as a plastic neon-coated sign." He stood on the balcony of the Fontainebleu Hotel in Miami Beach, the salty breeze from the Atlantic blowing hot and muggy at his back, the wisp of an Oriental—Chiun, the Master of Sinanju—exhorting heatedly at his front. Chiun's gracious flowing kimono was wrapped around his knees and came off his back like a yellow and red flag at rest. His thin white hair barely touched the neck of the gown. His back was to Remo.

He had just said, "One should not be forced to gaze constantly upon the wasted years of one's life." The "wasted years" he referred to was the time devoted to training Remo as the one and only assassin for CURE. Chiun had also muttered something in Korean, so quickly the words ran together, but Remo recognized it. It was the usual comment that even the Master of Sinanju was unable to transform mud into diamonds.

"There's no such thing as a plastic neon-coated sign," insisted Remo.

"I know, or you would have used it," said Chiun.

"I didn't have time."

"A fool is always in a hurry."

"I had several assignments that night."

"That is because you do not know how to deal with an emperor. You do not understand an emperor. You do not wish to understand an emperor. You wish to set fire to things. You wish to burn down things. Little children like to set fires to things, too. They like to see the pretty flames."

"But wasn't it you, Little Father, who told me that the secret of Sinanju was that it was beyond play-dancing, that it used everything?"

"Everything properly. Setting fire to property is not proper. Any fool can burn down a palace. Any fool can reap carnage upon a land. Any army can do that. If an emperor wants an assassin—" Chiun's voice quivered as if he were a priest referring to the original Twelve Apostles, his voice implying that one could find a fisherman or a tax collector anywhere, but an assassin, ah, that was someone special "—he seeks an assassin."

"I did what I had to do and I was glad I did it," said Remo angrily. "Fucking glad, if you want to know."

"Obscenity is the first sign of a man out of control," said Chiun.

"I heard you use obscenity once" Remo replied. "As a matter of fact, you use it very often. What do you call 'a pale piece of a pig's ear'?"

"You," said Chiun, who thought this response so humorous that he repeated the question and answer several times to his pupil, whose white man's sense of humor could not appreciate a joke of such subtlety.

"What do you call a pale piece of a pig's ear? You," said Chiun.

"I heard, I heard, I heard," said Remo. He headed for the door to the suite. They had been here four days and for four days he had endured this criticism and ridicule. During morning training, Chiun had asked Remo why he bothered to train when for a penny Remo could buy matches or for dollars a gun. Better yet, why didn't Remo get himself a bomb and drop it hither and yon? Preferably hither because if he aimed hither it would land yon. Like a disease, sloppiness led to more sloppiness, Chiun said.

Remo went out into the hot Miami day. He had long ago purged himself of his appetite for pizza, fatty corned beef, fried shrimp, and Chinese food loaded with monosodium glutamate. But sometimes when it was hot and a bar looked dark, damp and inviting, he thought wistfully of what it would be like to just walk in and order a foamy golden brew like anyone else. Just like anyone else. Which he wasn't.

He did not know when he had become different. He could not point to a day, or even a month or year. There was a time when he realized that after day after day of Chiun's training, guidance, prodding, and probing, his entire life was filled with hating the discipline while trying to achieve it—and there came that one moment when he realized he could never go back to what he had been. That he was someone else. And he had felt very frightened and very alone even though he could have, if he had wished, laid waste to every person he had seen that day, excepting Chiun himself, of course.

He felt as a newborn child must feel, but there were no arms to hold him and give him warmth and stroking;

there was only his discipline and the need to learn. He had not volunteered to learn. He had been hijacked into CURE by a man who had framed him for murder. And he had learned and learned and now he had a new life, and whether he liked it or not, it was his whole life.

As Chiun had said, "One does not ask for life. But it is all you have and you must live it and honor it and at the right time surrender it with the dignity and grace befitting the best that is in you."

And Remo had answered, "But Little Father, I thought all your training was so that I would not have to surrender my life."

"We all surrender life. It is the time and manner I hope to teach you. The fool sprinkles his life away like confetti upon the ground, a sacrifice to the passion of the moment. When your life goes, the very bowels of the earth will shake."

"And when your life goes?" Remo had asked.

"I had not thought of that yet. It is very far away. I am only in my eighth decade. But the way *your* training is progressing, I would think of it every day if I were you."

Remo stopped in front of a jewelry store. It was 11:05. He had ten minutes. At 11:15 there would be the weekly line open at Folcroft. The daily line had not yet answered. While Remo had never faced this problem before, he was sure that the weekly open line had to work. He believed it was much more secure because it was routed through Kansas City, up to Canada, and back down to Folcroft.

A frowsy blonde with a droopy print dress and perfume that would make a sewer snake retch asked Remo if he wanted honey for twenty dollars.

"No thanks," said Remo.

"Ten dollars. C'mon. It's a slow day. I'll clean your pipes."

"My pipes are clean."

"Five. I haven't done it for five since high school."

Remo shook his head. It was 11:12.

"I ain't doin' it for two. Five is the best price you can get."

"For what?"

"Me."

"Why would I want you?"

"You're queer, ain't you?"

"No," said Remo matter-of-factly and went off to a street telephone booth. The blonde followed.

"Look. I need the fast cash. Four. Four dollars, you should see a price like that again never."

"It's a good price," said Remo.

"A deal?"

"Sure," said Remo, reaching the phone booth. He slipped her a five. "I'll meet you around the corner in ten minutes. Don't run out on me."

She took the money, assuring him she wouldn't run out on such a handsome fellow. Which corner did he say?

"That one," said Remo, waving his left hand vaguely.

"You sure got big wrists."

"Runs in the family," said Remo.

"I don't have change."

"When I see you again, you give it to me."

It was 11:14. At the half-minute, Remo dialed. He heard the relays click, whine and gurgle, and then he heard the ringing.

The phone was answered mid-ring. Remo was surprised at how happy he was to hear even Smitty's voice. But it wasn't Dr. Harold Smith. Remo must have gotten the wrong number. He hung up quickly in hopes that he could still get in on the 11:15 line before it was

45

closed down. He dialed again, heard the clicking and waited. Three seconds, five seconds, seven seconds. Then the ring. And it was again answered mid-ring, but it was not Smith's voice.

"Who am I talking to?" asked Remo.

"New man in the office." The voice had that plastic California quality.

"Which office?"

"I believe the recipient of the phone call is supposed to do the asking. Who are you?"

"Is this Folcroft Sanitarium?"

"Yes."

"I must have a wrong line. I'm looking for Doctor Smith."

"He's on vacation. Can I help you?"

"No," said Remo.

"Look, fella, this is sort of a strange new job to me and you're coming in on a special line I have here. I gather you're sort of important. Now I think we're going to work together fine as soon as I get this project functioning along more effective directional lines. But you're going to have to work with me. I can tell you, I'm looking people over rather carefully."

"What are you talking about?"

"I'm asking who you are and what you do for us."

"Where's Dr. Smith?"

"I told you he's on vacation."

"Where?"

"There's a high-priority restriction on his place frame."

"Are you a person?" asked Remo, who had known what every one of the words meant, but could make no sense out of the sentence.

"I think you ought to come up to Folcroft and we'll have a little meeting, if you tell me who you are."

"You got a pen?" asked Remo.

"Yes."

"It's a long name."

"All right. Shoot."

Remo glanced across the street at a sign over a rug shop.

"Velspar Rombough Plekostian," he said, reading the sign. Remo spelled out the name two times, starting with "v" as in vasectomy and ending with "n" as in nut-nut.

"I don't see you listed in the personnel wrap-up."

"I'm there. You'll find me. Who are you?"

"Blake Corbish, I'm the new director here at the sanitarium."

"You've taken over all of Smith's duties?"

"All of them."

"I see," said Remo and hung up. There was something very wrong. No one but Smith was supposed to answer the weekly number. If something had happened to Smith, Remo was supposed to get a tape-recorded message from the computer on the line which would tell Remo what to do and how to contact Smith again, if ever. It was obvious that the computers had already been tampered with. But then only Smith knew the computers and that was probably because the cold-blooded unemotional Smith was related to them. One of them might have been his mother.

Remo did not know what to do. This would be important to Chiun, also, but Remo did not know whether or not to tell him that the House of Sinanju might have to seek a new employer.

It was possible that Smitty was dead. Perhaps a heart attack or an auto accident. Remo visualized a bloody Dr. Harold Smith in a mass of twisted auto wreckage. But to bleed, a man had to have blood in his veins. To have a heart attack required, first of all, a heart.

47

Smith wouldn't die. He wasn't that human.

Whatever happened, Remo intended to keep it from Chiun for a few days. The Master of Sinanju might be the master of many mysteries, but he was also somewhat unattuned to the Western world. His understanding of the West came only from television soap operas, and he sometimes had trouble telling the difference between a jet and a helicopter. He had often confused whole centuries and cultures, thinking of the Russians as good because their czars paid well and overestimating the importance of a small African tribe because the House of Sinanju had rendered services to them before the time of Christ.

Remo planned to return to the hotel suite, perhaps read a magazine and think in peace, and figure out their next moves.

A frowsy blonde waved at him from the corner. It was the hooker.

"Hi, I've been waiting."

"I thought you were supposed to walk with the money. All hookers do."

"For you, I'd wait."

"There's a rug merchant down the block who could use you. Pays good too. His name's Velspar Rombough Plekostian. Twenty bucks, guaranted."

The hooker's face brightened and she followed Remo's finger.

Well, though Remo, into each life some rain must fall. Because this rug merchant had a sign outside his shop with his name, he would soon be under investigation by a secret agency and plagued by the overperfumed attentions of a hooker.

But then life was never fair, and if Remo hadn't been an orphan and had not been seen in Vietnam by one of Smith's operatives, and if, and if, and if . . . Life

48

was not fair for Remo Williams, nor was it fair for Velspar Rombough Plekostian, although Remo thought, he liked Velspar's name better.

When Remo entered the suite, he heard the low, whiney conversation of the daytime soaps. Remo was careful not to walk in front of Dr. Rance Remerow who was talking to Mrs. Jeri Tredmore about Mrs. Tredmore's daughter who was dying of leukemia while about to give birth to a baby everyone believed sired by someone other than her husband, perhaps by Bruce Wilson, the noted black nuclear physicist who was torn between working for science or for Black Revolution.

Remo remembered one scene in passing because Dr. Bruce Wilson, the noted nuclear physicist, had been referring to "bofe nuchrons" when he meant "both neutrons." This was somewhat better that Dr. Remerow who referred to netrones and Mrs. Tredmore who twice referred to neuters.

Chiun watched all of this in rapture, and Remo for the first time felt grateful that these shows absorbed Chiun's attention, while Remo thought.

When the last commercial faded into the afternoon movies, Remo strolled casually through the parlor of the suite, looking for the phone to call room service for rice and fish, no sauces, no spices, no butter. Boiled rice and only slightly warmed fish.

"We must talk about your deep troubles," said Chiun.

"What troubles?" said Remo with a casual shrug.

"The trouble that has been bothering you since you returned."

"No trouble," said Remo, as he dialed the base of the table lamp and waited for the shade to say hello.

CHAPTER FIVE

Chiun gave the problem much thought. Indeed, he said, they both had a problem. An emperor's fall, if it should be a fall, was a serious thing. People might start thinking, even though they might not say it, that the House of Sinanju was responsible for the emperor's fall, that this Emperor Smith had hired the House of Sinanju and look, there he is, dead.

But this would not be fair because the House of Sinanju had been hired only to train for Emperor Smith. But would people know that? The problem both Remo and Chiun now faced was explaining that the House of Sinanju had been hired only to train personnel and that if Sinanju had been commissioned to serve fully, which it had not, Smith would be alive and well today, ruling peacefully and sublime.

"That's not exactly the problem, Little Father," said Remo.

Chiun looked puzzled.

"What else could be the problem?"

"I don't know what's happened to Smith. I just believe he has been injured or killed."

"Then why not go to the palace and find out?"

"Because I am under orders never to return to Folcroft where you first trained me. I'm not supposed to be connected with that place. I've never been able to get this through to you. Smith's organization is not supposed to exist."

"Congratulations," said Chiun. He sat in a lotus position on the floor while Remo sat on the couch.

"On what?"

"Once again not getting that through to me. I do not understand. Smith is most inscrutable. No palace guards. No concubines. No servants. No treasures. Ah, the mysteries of the West. Smith was a mad emperor whom the House of Sinanju could not save from his madness. That is it. The world will understand that."

Remo got up from the couch and paced. "Only half a dozen people in the world have ever heard of Sinanju and they don't talk, so that's not our problem," he said.

"Then what is our problem? We will always find work. When the world has no more use for artists or doctors or scientists or philosophers, it will still need good assassins. Do not worry. A crazy Western emperor will not hurt our reputation."

"This is going to be very hard to explain, Little Father. But I love my country. Smith was not my emperor. We both served another emperor and that was the country. If CURE, Smith's organization, still serves this nation, then I wish to continue serving CURE."

"On your back," said Chiun. "Quickly."

Remo dropped to the floor and flattened on his back.

"Take the air to the very essence of yourself. Hold. Hold it. Hold the air and live on your will. Emit the air. Live on your will. Your organs slow now. Your heart slows. Only your will survives. Now. Snap. The air. Snap the air. In far. Out far. Much air."

Remo felt his very mind bathed in freshness and light. He sat up and smiled.

"Do you feel better now?"

"Yes," said Remo.

"It is a good thing. You were beginning to talk the madness of the mad Emperor Smith."

Remo threw up his hands. "Let me explain it this way, Little Father. If there is a new emperor, I wish to serve him. I'm an American."

"I never held that against you. There are some very nice Americans."

"I will serve this new emperor," Remo said. "I hope you will, too."

Chiun slowly shook his aged head.

"First, what right have you to take the gift of the teachings of Sinanju and squander it? What right do you have to take the years I gave you and cast them at the feet of any unknown?"

"You were paid, Little Father."

"I was paid to teach you killing tricks, not Sinanju as I have taught you. What I gave was a gift from many generations of Masters of Sinanju. Before what you call your ancient Rome, we were. Before that mud swamp barbarian village on the Seine, Paris, we were. Before the island people of Britain, we were. When the Hebrews wandered in the desert, we had a home and we knew the discipline of Sinanju. You have been given Sinanju, not because your emperor's coin, or your country, or any contract your mind can conceive demanded it, but because you, Remo Williams, were a vessel worthy to receive it."

Remo stopped pacing. He stood motionless on the

rug. He felt the words come hard and felt strange tears form behind his eyes.

"Me, Little Father. Worthy?"

"For a white man," said Chiun, lest his pupil run amok at such praise and succumb to arrogance, the one impenetrable barrier against wisdom.

"I . . . I . . ."

Remo was speechless.

"Secondly," said Chiun, for he too felt things he did not wish to express, "you cannot serve another emperor. No Master of Sinanju serves a succeeding emperor. For this, there are good reasons. One, people might say the Master arranged the death of the first emperor. Secondly, and this you may not understand for many years, for you are not even four decades old yet, but a new emperor buries the sword of his predecessor."

"I don't understand, Chiun."

"A new emperor wants his own power. It does not happen today, but when ancient rulers died, they were often buried with their most trusted and highly placed ministers. This was not as some have come to believe so they could serve him in another world. No, it was because the new emperor or pharoah or khan, or whatever men wish to call a president or chairman or czar— because truly they are all alike—it is because the new emperor does not wish other powers than his to be present. Today, a new emperor comes to power and the servants of the old emperor retire, which is a different form of death. But in our world, they must die, as was the way in the past. You cannot serve the new emperor because he does not want you around. He wants his own ministers. This I know."

"We don't work like that in America. This isn't the Orient or 1,200 B.C. This is America in the twentieth century."

"And your country is inhabited by human beings?"

"Of course."

"Then your country is the same. You are just not wise enough to perceive what I tell you, because you are a little baby still short of four decades of life."

"You've made my mind up for me," Remo said. "I'm going to Folcroft."

"I will go with you for you carry more than a decade of my life and we have a saying in Sinanju that babies should not wander the streets alone."

"I wonder when your ancestors ever had time for training," said Remo angrily. "You're so damned busy shooting off your mouth with sayings for this and sayings for that. You ought to go on television like that social worker in the funny Western hat."

"I know the one," said the Mastor of Sinanju. "Kung Fu. The white man whose eyes are made to look normal."

What Remo did not consider, and what many Americans had never conceived, was that America did have royalty. Not bestowed by accident of womb, but by personal accomplishment—by inventing, discovering, creating, or performing.

And a true lord of the nobility of merit spit the blood from his aging mouth, tried to focus eyes that had been filled with tears of torture, and sat up in the lead-lined basement of a hilltop house near Bolinas, California.

He did not know where he was, not even the continent for sure, or even the week or month. He knew his body was covered by painful welts, that his right leg had suffered nerve damage, and that breathing itself was very hard. But as he swallowed the water that felt like razor blades going down his throat, he knew one more very important thing. His adversary had made an incredible blunder. Dr. Harold W. Smith was alive.

He should not have been alive, not at his age, not after the shock to his body. But he had been reared in the Vermont countryside where winters whipped physical hardship upon a young boy who had wanted above all things to be a lawyer, then a judge. In school, when others cheated on exams, Harold Smith covered his paper, even when he sat next to the class bully. As he had tried to explain to the much larger boy, he would be doing him no favor by helping him through school painlessly. The struggle to learn was part of the growing up process, young Harold had said.

The bully took a much simpler view of cheating. He didn't want any lip from Harold Smith, he wanted the answers. He would get the answers or Harold would get a bloody nose. Nobody, not even his parents, called Harold Smith Harry. It was always Harold. He was somber, even in diapers.

The whole class gathered around to watch Harold get his. Get it, he did. A bloody nose the first day. A black eye the second. A chipped tooth the third. On the fourth day, the class bully explained he did not want to fight after school anymore. If Harold didn't want to give him the answers, then Harold could keep his old answers. Who needed them anyway?

Harold reminded him there was unfinished business. He drew a dusty line with his shoe in the school yard and dared the bully to cross it. The bully did and decked Harold again. By this time the class sympathy had shifted in favor of the school wet blanket against the bully, who tried to explain that it was Harold who started the fight this time.

For five more days, every day at the end of school, Harold and the bully fought. On the fifth day, Harold got in a good right cross to the bully's nose. It bled. The bully cried. And gave up.

No one picked on Harold again. He wasn't worth it.

When he was fourteen Harold met Maude. She lived in neighboring Windham. They were married thirteen years later after a courtship so dull, she later confesssed to a friend, that Maude felt they were ready for their golden wedding anniversary celebration halfway through their first date. The date was to a Marx Brothers movie at which Harold not only failed to laugh but kept interrupting to point out that Groucho's moustache was painted on and for fifteen cents the least the movie company could do would be to give them a man with a real moustache.

Harold even had the ability to make his Congregationalist minister, the Rev. Jesse Rolfe Prescott, feel like justifying himself when he said hello. There was an aura about Harold Smith of relentless integrity.

He got a full scholarship to Dartmouth, went on to Harvard Law, got his doctorate, and was teaching law at Yale when World War II broke out. Everyone thought he would be a natural for the inspector general's office. Everyone except Wild Bill Donovan of the OSS who had an uncanny ability to see talent where others failed to even suspect it.

Against the high-booted Nazi SS, with their testicle crushers and ceremonial daggers, the honest boy from Vermont cut a swath like a flamethrower through a spider web. By the third year of the war, he had agents placed high in their command. He compromised the Gestapo. It was the classic case of the diligent worker versus the emotionally involved sadist. Workers always won.

The law professor from Yale had found a vocation he had never sought or even dreamed of. When the OSS retooled to emerge as the CIA for the cold war, Harold Smith was in a high command position. He had the reputation of getting things done successfully and quietly.

He never confided to anyone why he stayed because no one ever asked. While he longed to return to Yale, he felt he owed it to his country to remain in the CIA, mainly to keep the zanies, as he called them, from mucking things up. The zanies had plans for everything, from kidnapping Mao Tse-tung and replacing him with a double, to setting off a thermonuclear explosion at Magnetogor as a way of convincing the Russians that it was not safe to stockpile nuclear weapons.

Harold fervently hoped there were men in Russia and China to keep their zanies in line also. If Harold Smith had a prayer for the human race, it was:

"Lord, save us from those with dramatic solutions."

One month he noticed he was being checked out as thoroughly as if he had never had security clearance. The investigation, as he would later find out, having access to FBI files, had even interviewed the bully from school days who was now an assistant school principal.

"The finest fellow I ever knew," was the bully's comment. "Had a good right cross. Became a lawyer, went off to teach at Yale and we never heard from him again."

Maude's comment was: "Lacks imagination."

The dean of Yale Law School said: "Rather dull, but brilliant too. He reminds me of Dimaggio in centerfield. He does the difficult so routinely, he makes it look easy."

"I don't remember him, unless he was that somber little fellow who criticized our Sunday School for being too frivolous," said Reverend Prescott.

"Somewhat backward in the social amenities. We were worried about him for a while but fortunately he found that lovely girl from Windham," said Nathan Smith, Harold's father.

"Harold always was a good boy," said Mrs. Nathan Smith, Harold's mother.

"Who?" asked SS Obengrupper Fuehrer Heinz Raucht, whose special commando units had been rendered ineffective for the last two years of Warld War II by Operation Plum Bob, Col. Harold Smith, commanding.

"A prick," stated Agent Conrad MacCleary, transferred from European to Asian Theater during World War II for drunkenness, recklessness and gross insubordination. "But a fair prick. Balls to spare. Toughest thin-lipped son of a bitch I ever met."

The investigation into Harold Smith's background led to one job. The most important job of his life, a job that terrified him by the enormity of its prospects.

"Why me, Mr. President?" asked Harold Smith. "Out of 180 million people, there must be someone better."

"You're the someone, Smith. I trust you with a nation's future."

"It's unconstitutional, Mr. President," Smith had said. "As a matter of fact, we are both violating the law by even discussing this. And I'm not all that sure that I won't make a citizen's arrest right here in the White House."

The young president had smiled an engaging politician's smile, a smile that had absolutely no effect on Harold Smith, who had heard an impropriety of the grossest order.

"I'm glad you said that, Smith. I'm not even going to ask you not to do what you have just proposed. I'm going to ask you to think for a week. You know the law. You taught it. You think about whether this cherished constitution can survive. We are facing a trial as a nation, the hope for a kind of government that man has never really known in his history, that we have never faced before. I don't think the constitution is going to survive. I think you've got to violate it to save it. It's that simple."

"Or that complicated," said Smith. In a week he thought and prayed enough for a lifetime, hoping that this task would pass from him, that he would not have to assume this awful power. "If not me, who?" he wondered unhappily. "If not CURE, what?" And with fear and humility he had agreed, but he refused to shake the President's hand.

Now someone else, an outsider, was trying to take over the power of CURE. He might very well have it in his grasp already.

Smith took another long drink of water. It went down with less pain. He heard nothing in the lead room but his heavy breathing. They had not left him much strength, but they had left him his mind.

He looked at the table he was on. The straps hung uselessly at its side. His own blood was on them. The walls of the place were curiously familiar. A bomb shelter. There were two kinds of people who would build a shelter. A military operation or a private individual afraid of nuclear war. Now, if this were a military post, there was nothing much Harold Smith could do for the moment. But if a private individual had constructed this place, a man who was obviously insecure, then there just might be something, then there probably *was* something.

A frightened man would visualize himself in this chamber during a nuclear attack. He would see himself in a cellar with the world around him in ruins. He certainly wouldn't want this room to be his coffin. Supposing a beam from the roof above this room, or suppose even a boulder, were to fall on the door? He could not open it himself. He would be trapped. He who sees nuclear wars also sees their aftermath.

The man who had built this shelter would not be

content to die there just because he could not open the door to get out.

Smith looked around; he noticed a small box on a nearby wall. It had numbers and appeared to be a thermostat for the heating and cooling system. It was the only break in the smooth, gray dullness of the walls.

Smith steadied himself and tried to stand. He tumbled, his elbow knocking over a water glass. A small cut. He hardly felt it. By comparison to the rest of his pain, it was only a minor annoyance. Blood flowed from his elbow. He examined the wound with his fingertips looking for the little gurgle that would show a vein had been punctured. There was none. Good. He crawled to the box. His right leg did not work correctly, and he had to drag it behind him, even though dragging shot paralyzing pain through the broken, burned, electrically singed skin. He rested beneath the box, then summoning all his energy and using the wall as a brace, he got to his knees.

He felt the box and his hand searched for a button or a lever. There was none. He pulled open the door of the thermostat and felt inside. There was a small thumb-sized hook which he grabbed and pulled. He heard a whirring and a grinding, but nothing moved. Nowhere in the room did a door open. He felt a lightness in his head and then everything became dark. When he awoke, his cheek was against the side of the lead wall. The box was above him. Mucous and blood had formed near his mouth during unconsciousness. His cheek was caked with it. He tried to lift himself and this time it was easier. He was beyond pain now and beyond tiredness, observing his failing muscles the way a dispassionate coach might judge a lineman to see what he might be able to do in the upcoming season.

Apart from the right leg, his other parts seemed to

60

work, although his sight was still fuzzy and his stomach muscles were in disarray, and he was surprised at how much they were needed to stand up straight. But stand he did, for his legs supported him, even though his right leg felt as if it were made of skin stuffed with wet cloths, and then bless them, they moved and he moved with them, and he was able to walk a little.

He made his way to the far wall, and there he saw what had made the whirring, grinding sound before he passed out. A lead panel had slid open and inside it, he saw a large plunger like the terminal of a three-foot-wide syringe. He threw his body against it, and with a cracking sound, a big, wide beautiful square of light opened up as the door rolled slowly into the room, pushing Harold Smith aside on legs that somehow managed to keep him upright. The fresh air was like a bath of light. He waited and heard nothing. Bent over, he made his way up a short staircase, three painful steps to a wall of wood. He pushed and the wall gave way. And then he was in a living room with a magnificent view and he saw or heard no other person. He was alone. Through a large ceiling-high window, he saw a sun set red over a large body of lapping water. It was an ocean. If it were the Atlantic, he was in Europe. If it were the Pacific, he was still in America. All he remembered was offering a piece of paper to Blake Corbish, just one of the many IDC people he had been watching. Then he had awakened to the never-ending pain.

Smith saw the electrical outlets in the wall. Many of them. America, it must be America. The house was on the side of a hill and down the road he could see a little white cabin. Something was strange about the windows. Hazily, he saw they were boarded up. He saw a phone near him. Outside, a wire hung limp against a pole. If the phone was dead, then it was likely that no one

61

had been left on guard. The dead phones were obviously a precaution. With great effort, Smith knocked the receiver off the cradle. He listened but heard nothing. No dial tone. Just silence.

Smith turned toward the window. Then, dragging his right leg behind him, he began to move, painfully, slowly. Even as he moved, he was planning his counterattack.

CHAPTER SIX

A commodities broker who had once been caught embezzling and had been forgiven provided he reported every day the tidbits of gossip that swirled around the Chicago Exchange like wheat chaff in a storm, was suddenly was asked to report on different things. Not only was he required to relay information as usual on any movements of large amounts of cash and brokerage infighting, but now he was ordered to supply the kind of inside information from which people could make fortunes, the kind of information he dare not use himself lest he lose his license.

A Teamster official who had been keeping tabs on organized crime in the trucking business, now found out that the extra monthly stipend he received required advance information on contract demands.

And a federal judge was told point-blank that the Internal Revenue Service had discovered grave discrepancies in his returns, though some things could be overlooked for the good of the country. It was explained to this judge, as he sat in his chambers in a Phoenix courthouse, that America needed a strong International Data Corporation, just as it needed good judges. The judge must decide he could not find against IDC in a monopoly suit brought by a smaller computer firm. A decision against IDC could wreck the nation's whole economy. The country was, of course, willing to forgive him his unreported extra income if he would help the country. Hardly pausing for breath, he proved himself a true patriot.

These accomplishments were the first in what Blake Corbish was sure would be a delightful series of successes. Blake Corbish considered them and whistled a pleasant tune as he drove a pickup truck up the winding hillside road to the estate outside Bolinas, California.

He had told his secretary back at Folcroft that he needed a rest. Some physical exercise and he would be back in a day. Any messages for him could be left at IDC headquarters in Mamaroneck, or he could be reached the following morning at the Manhattan offices of T. L. Broon, president and chairman of the board of IDC.

"You seem to do an awful lot of business with IDC, Mr. Corbish," the secretary had said.

"We have a heavy computer commitment here at Folcroft."

"Dr. Smith never had that many computer people around," said the secretary.

Blake Corbish had smiled and said that a new broom sweeps clean. The nosey little biddy had been transferred to the cafeteria before his car had cleared the grounds.

The rattle of bricks and tin in the rear of his pickup was a reassuring sound. It said Blake Corbish, vice president, Blake Corbish, senior vice president for policy planning, Blake Corbish, president, Blake Corbish, chairman of the board. And as he passed the boarded-up white cabin, it said something else: Blake Corbish, President of the United States.

Why not? Why not Blake Corbish? The ranging blue of the California sky reminded him of how far he had come, how many times he had been close to failure and had toughed it out. Like high school. They had been giving scholarships to the raving little geniuses or the hulking athletes. His parents were not poor enough to qualify him for aid on the basis of need, and not rich enough to afford to pay tuition at Williams, a not-quite Ivy League school where one could nevertheless launch a career. So Blake Corbish had joined extracurricular activities. Committees, plays, social events, school projects, he was there. But when he found out in his senior year that it would not be enough, Blake Corbish ran for class president and worked at being liked. His opponent had been one of those zanies that people are naturally attracted to. Running against him threatened to make the school election into a popularity contest, which in later analysis, Corbish realized all school elections were. But this one had seemed more important at the time, important enough to call his supporters to a private meeting and sincerely plead with them *not* to spread the gossip that his opponent was a thief who stole watches from the gym lockers.

"I don't want to win if I have to win that way," said Corbish. Naturally the unfounded rumor spread through the school. In approximately an hour it had become such widespread knowledge that after much audible soul searching Blake Corbish had found it necessary to publicly plead with the senior class not to let the personal lives of the candidates unduly influence their votes.

Corbish won by a landslide. He got his scholarship to Williams, finishing 73rd in a class of 125. As one pro-

65

fessor described him, he was "an incredibly undistinguished scholar whose morality reflected social convenience rather than any sense of right or wrong, a man who could throw people into ovens as easily as he might work to support the Salvation Army, making no distinction between them."

Why not President of the United States? thought Blake Corbish. After all, who would have suspected Blake Corbish of Mendocino, California, would become the youngest senior vice president for policy planning in the history of IDC?

When Corbish parked the truck in the small driveway he noted that the kitchen door was ajar. Had someone entered the house? He could have sworn he locked it, and the old man had to be dead by now. He checked the back of the pickup. The bricks and cement were in fine order. Within a month or two, it wouldn't matter if the body were found. If he continued at Folcroft the way he had started, in a month he could get the person who found Dr. Smith's body convicted of the crime. He could do anything.

But right now he had to handle the sticky details. And there were many of them. For instance, the direct line from the President of the United States to Smith's desk. Corbish had made a tape recording and cut it into the line. The recording said simply that there was transmission trouble on the line. The call would be returned. This was just a holding action, but it would keep the President out of it until Corbish had gotten all of CURE and Folcroft under his control.

There were many similar details which Corbish had to handle. And when they were done, he would be able to use the power of CURE in any way he wanted. Why not President of the United States?

Corbish had intended to return sooner for Smith, but

when he discovered that the old man had indeed given him the correct programming instructions, he tossed himself into his work with the glee of a child playing with a new set of toys. One day led to another and then another and then another. Day after day of successful operations. Now it was too late. So be it. Smith would already be dead. Corbish had learned from the computers that Smith had been investigating Blake Corbish and that meant Smith planned to have him killed. It was just Smith's bad luck that Corbish had been smarter.

Corbish saw dark stains on the kitchen floor. He bent to examine them. He scratched one with his thumb. It crinkled like a nut frosting. Bloodstains. Several days old. They came from the living room. In the living room, he saw they came from a passageway behind a bookcase. The passageway, he saw, led to the lead-lined room.

And the room was empty.

He felt the first rushes of panic overcome him and he subdued them. He had been in tight spots before. All right, Smith had escaped. Reasonable. He was also very weak. Was it possible someone had come to rescue him?

Corbish looked at the stains. Doubtful. You don't rescue someone in Smith's condition and let him bleed all the way to the door.

No, the old man had somehow found the energy to escape. By himself.

All right. What could Smith do? He could contact his killer arm. Corbish thought about the long winding road, the isolation of the area, and, most blessedly, the dismantled telephone line. But the stains were days old. If Smith had contacted the killer arm, Corbish would have been dead by now. And he was very much alive.

All right, this is where the successes are separated from the failures. He would tough it out.

Corbish did not have to brick up the deep basement anymore so he drove back into town, every once in a while braking the increasing speed that came when he brooded about the empty cellar. The bricks rattled loudly in the back of the truck, but none bounced out. By the time Corbish was at his Manhattan appointment with T.L. Broon on the other side of the country, he was smiling confidently, assured, gracious and rather humble as praise was heaped upon the youngest senior vice president for policy planning in the history of International Data Corporation.

He spoke before the executive committee of IDC— nine men who looked remarkably like Blake Corbish and T.L. Broon himself—and before T.L. Broon's father, whose portrait hung in the Manhattan boardroom, a pastel-carpeted expanse of low-ceilinged space with indirect lighting and a table so long and so wide it made everyone sitting at the sides feel insignificant. Only the person at the head of the table could feel he mattered. And that, Corbish reflected, was T.L. Broon. At least for the moment.

Only one face in the door did not exude dynamic optimism. It was the portrait of Josiah Broon, who had started IDC with a sales route for a cash register that was much like all other cash registers, until Josiah came up with the slogan, "It thinks for you." As more and more executives realized the dangers of doing any sort of thinking at all, at least any that could be traced to them, IDC grew and became a giant.

The expression of old Josiah looked down on the boardroom as if someone had created an unpleasant odor. It was much the same expression he had worn in life and had worn when he transferred the company to T.L. Broon.

"I don't think even you can fuck it up, sonny. We're too rich for that now."

In the published history of IDC, these words mellowed, with the help of the public relations department, until they became: "You represent, son, what is best in America."

Those words were engraved in a bronze plaque beneath the portrait of Josiah before which Blake Corbish now spoke.

"I accept this promotion on behalf of the IDC team," said Corbish. "IDC always has meant the future and the future is youth."

There were smiles and applause around the table. Corbish reveled in the insincerity of the smiles because here insincerity was the sincerest form of compliment. If youth was the future, then these members of the executive board were the past.

Broon called Corbish to the head of the table and shook his hand.

"You are now senior vice president for policy planning," said Broon.

And it was done.

Senior Vice President Blake Corbish. Who would have thought it? Blake Corbish from Mendocino, California. And maybe one day, President of the United States Blake Corbish.

Of course, there were still some obstacles. One of them was at that moment in a San Francisco hospital, insisting that he not only felt good enough to walk, but to make a phone call himself.

He dialed a Miami hotel.

"I'm sorry, sir. That party has checked out," said the operator to Dr. Harold Smith.

CHAPTER SEVEN

There were guards now at Folcroft, young men with neat snappy uniforms and polished black holsters who stopped people at the entrance to examine identification. Remo noticed that only those with little printed badges that glowed purple under a scanner were allowed to pass.

Camera eyes scanned the old brick walls of the one-time estate.

"It doesn't look the same," said Remo. "Not just the guards and the cameras, but the walls don't look as I remember them. They used to seem so big and thick and impenetrable."

"This is not the same place you left, because you are now different," said Chiun.

"I guess so," said Remo.

"The weather in Persia must be beautiful at this time of year. Have you ever tasted melon at the very moment of ripening? It is one of the truly rare fruits."

"It's Iran, now, Little Father," said Remo, who had been fielding these suggestions since Miami. First, it had been Russia. The czars always paid reliably and generously, Czar Ivan being the finest.

"You mean, Ivan the Terrible?" asked Remo.

"Terrible for whom?" Chiun had answered. He suggested that perhaps one of those new South American countries might have the proper need and respect for an assassin of the caliber of Sinanju. Why, Remo and Chiun could make economic history by opening up these markets. They could always train Samurai, and incidentally, keep them in line for the emperor, who had always had trouble with the Samurai which was the real reason why centuries ago the throne of the White Camelia had declared itself divine—to place some fear in the hearts of the wild bandit Samurai. An undisciplined wild country was Japan, with many bandits roaming the mountains.

Thus spoke the Master of Sinanju who said he was even now receiving correspondence through the American postal system at a post office box in the northeast, and who knew, one day it might bring him and Remo a job offer.

Remo looked at the camera eyes on top of Folcroft which, like most scanners, left areas uncovered for brief moments. Ordinarily, this would be good-enough protection, especially on a high wall such as Folcroft's.

Before a camera caught them, Remo and Chiun were over the wall and down into the vast lawny courtyard smelling of spring blossoms. Chiun commented that the blossoms here were nothing compared to the blossoms of the courtyard of the moguls of Jodhpur.

The administration building still had the one-way windows facing the Long Island Sound which was as nothing compared to the beauty of the Bay of Bengal.

The ledges near the one-way windows were pathetic brick outcroppings compared to the temples of Rome.

And there was supposed to be a new temple in Rome greater than all the others. This recent architectural sensation, Remo discovered upon questioning, was St. Peter's.

Remo and Chiun worked themselves flat against a large gray moulding encrusted with bird droppings. They could hear voices in nearby windows but not from the one-way window.

They entered through a clear window, excused themselves to startled secretaries, pushed through two doors until they were in the office that looked out on the Sound through the one-way glass.

A blondish man in a neat gray suit, white shirt and not-too-wide tie was conducting a meeting at a long conference table. The other men were dressed remarkably like him, almost as if they were in uniform. The blondish man was in his late thirties and he looked upon the aged Oriental and the taller white man with some confusion and much indignation, but before he could speak, he was spoken to.

"Who the hell are you?" asked Remo.

"I was just about to ask you that," said Blake Corbish.

"None of your business. Who are these dingalings?" asked Remo, pointing to the new executive staff coordinating committee of Folcroft, presently composed of IDC executives on loan to Corbish.

"I beg your pardon," said Corbish, who reached under the long table to press a buzzer, but suddenly saw the intruder move very close to him and then felt his fingers go numb.

"You're the new director of Folcroft, right?" said Remo.

"Yes," said Corbish wincing. The other executives said they had never seen an impropriety such as this before.

The Oriental informed them that he who sees disturbing things perhaps has no need of eyes.

"C'mon, old fella," said the assistant coordinating director of programming, a former tight end for Purdue, trying to be gentle with the frail old Oriental in the wispy kimono. He placed a friendly hand on the old man's bony shoulder. At least he thought he placed a friendly hand on the bony shoulder. He remembered it going down to the shoulder and then he saw tubes coming out of his nose, bright lights above his head and heard a doctor reassuring him he would live, and in all probability, even walk again.

When the assistant coordinating director went down in a massive heap at the feet of the Oriental, it was decided by the executive staff coordinating committee that the meeting should be adjourned and that the director of Folcroft, Blake Corbish, should conduct a private interview with the two guests of the sanitarium. The vote was taken by feet moving rapidly to the door and it was unanimous. Shortly thereafter, five guards came running into director Corbish's office to see what the commotion was about. They too agreed that private meetings should be kept private. This agreement was reached so amiably that four of them were able to leave under their own power.

Blake Corbish smiled very sincerely.

"You must be Williams, Remo," he said. "Smith told me a lot about you before the accident."

"This man is backwards," Chiun whispered to Remo.

"What accident?" said Remo.

"I guess you couldn't have known," said Corbish with a forthright look of concern on his face. "Please sit down. You too, sir. If I'm correct, you also are an employee. Sinanju, Master of."

"The Master of Sinanju is never a servant. He is a respected ally who receives tribute," Chiun said.

"I'm glad you could see your way to making your way here, sir, since we're in the process of reorganization and we've noticed some unusual expenses relating to your employment, I mean, your profile as respected ally."

"What happened to Smith?" asked Remo. His voice was lead heavy.

"That later," said Chiun. "Important matters first. Explain yourself, you."

"Who's first?" said Corbish. He felt sensation return to his fingertips like the buzzing of fresh soda pop. His shirt had become wet with perspiration.

"I'm first," said Chiun.

"What happened to Smith?" said Remo.

"Let him do one thing at a time," Chiun said to Remo. "Even that which appears simultaneous is one thing at a time."

"Thank you," said Corbish.

"The expenses," said Chiun.

Corbish ordered a printout by voice over an intercom. This seemed very suspicious to Remo, since when Smith had run things, only he himself had had access to the organization's printouts.

The expenses Corbish referred to were the cost of the delivery of gold to the village of Sinanju in North Korea, approximately 175 times the value of the gold itself. Now this wasn't sound business planning. Why not take delivery here in the States and Corbish could see his way clear to doubling the annual tribute?

"No," said Chiun.

"I'll triple it," said Corbish.

"No," said Chiun. "The gold must go to Sinanju."

"Perhaps we could mail dollars."

"Deliver gold," Chiun said.

74

"Then we have another item, a special television device that records simultaneous shows I gather, then feeds them back consecutively into a single television set. The explanation has something to do with soap operas, I believe."

"Correct."

"Would it be possible to have tapes mailed to you, sir? It would really be much less expensive."

"No," said Chiun.

"Well, I'm glad we've settled that," said Corbish.

"What about Smith?" said Remo. He noticed that Chiun, who had railed against serving a succeeding emperor, now seemed satisfied. Chiun placed himself on the floor in a full lotus position and with barely casual curiosity observed the goings-on.

"Your instructor's profile prohibits his participation in these matters."

"He doesn't understand what's going on anyhow. He thinks of Smith as an emperor. He's all right," Remo said.

"As you know," said Corbish somberly, "this is a very delicate organization. You are one of the three men, I guess now four, who knows specifically what we are about. These are hard times and it is a hard thing I must tell you. Dr. Smith—perhaps it was the pressure of the job, I don't know—but Dr. Smith suffered a nervous breakdown a week ago. He fled the sanitarium and has not been heard from since."

"But why you in his place?" said Remo. He rested a hand on the new long conference table that butted up against Smith's old desk.

"Because you failed, Williams. Your assignment, according to your employment profile, was, if Smith showed mental aberrations, to kill him. Now did you or did you not observe that he was deteriorating?"

"I saw some unusual things but he's often ordered unusual things."

"Like terminating an employee strata of a major American corporation? Didn't you question his actions?"

"I was too busy."

"You were too busy following his demented instructions, Williams. What you have literally done is fail your country. This organization was set up with enough checks and balances so that if any move were made to endanger this country through this organization, it would begin to disband. You know that. Your job was to kill Smith. I believe when he was sane he personally gave you those instructions. Am I correct?"

"Yes."

"Why didn't you?" asked Corbish.

"I wasn't sure he'd lost his marbles," said Remo.

"That's not so, is it?"

"Well, I knew he was under a lot of pressure."

"You knew you didn't want to kill him, isn't that so?" Corbish said.

"Yeah, I guess it is," said Remo.

"That makes you unreliable, doesn't it?"

"I guess so," said Remo.

"What do you think I ought to do about it?"

"Try pissing up a rope," said Remo.

Chiun emitted a cackle. Corbish nodded solemnly. He talked about a nation struggling for its survival. He talked about each man doing his duty. He talked about Remo's life and he talked about many lives. He said he could not force Remo to help undo the damage of Smith's last months. But he said he was going to go ahead by himself and try to return the organization back to its original objectives. That was how Smith, in his saner moments, would have wanted it.

Remo felt old stirrings of allegiance that he thought

were long since gone. He glanced at Chiun. In Korean, the Master of Sinanju had one word: "bird droppings."

"Who appointed you?" Remo asked Corbish.

"The same person who appointed Smith. Frankly, I didn't want this job. I saw what it did to Smith. I think it might do that to me. If you should decide to continue to work for us, I would hope that before I deteriorated like Dr. Smith has, you would do your duty properly and prevent me from causing the severe sort of damage Smith did in his last days."

"Bird droppings," said Chiun again in Korean but Remo ignored him. Chiun had never understood the love of country or loyalty to a cause, considering them a waste of talent. Well, so be it. That was the Master of Sinanju. He had been trained since childhood to think that way. But Remo was an American and there still lingered in him an ember of childhood patriotism that would not die no matter how he changed. Looking at this man who had replaced Smith, Remo thought that he just might give this man and his country another chance.

Corbish apparently was not as rigid as Smith. Remo realized that he had come to think of the organization as Smith's, that he had incorrectly believed it could not exist without the parsimonious old wet blanket. Maybe it would even be better with this man who seemed to be more reasonable than Smith, and definitely less fidgety.

"I'd like to think a few moments," said Remo.

"Yes," said Chiun in English. "He wants to exercise muscles never used before."

"I think you're the kind of man we need on the team," said Corbish.

"I think I'm going to be unable to eat for a month," said Chiun.

Corbish left his office to Remo and went outside.

"Little Father," said Remo, "I must at least try."

"Of course," said Chiun. "You have nothing invested in you. Minimal talent and less energy. *I* have created you. *I* have a great investment."

"I appreciate what you have done for me, but I also have other loyalties. I think I can trust this man. He may even be an improvement over Smith."

"The second emperor buries the sword of the first," said Chiun.

"If that's so, why does Corbish want me to continue?"

"What makes you think he does?"

"He just asked me. Didn't you hear?"

"I heard," said Chiun.

"I'm going to give it a shot," said Remo. "I'm going to see what happens."

"With my gift of wisdom," said Chiun disdainfully.

"Your village will be supported. The gold will get there to care for the elderly and the orphans. You have no worries, no worries at all," said Remo.

"Bird droppings," said the Master of Sinanju.

CHAPTER EIGHT

In previous corporate battles, there had been memoranda, positions to be taken, charts to show one's corporate posture to be superior to another's, sales progress, corporate responsibility well accepted.

Blake Corbish looked around his home den, examined his own corporate resources, and said:

"Bullshit. I don't have to wait for anyone anymore."

"What did you say?" asked Teri Corbish, a sandy-haired young woman in high turtleneck sweater and full, cleanly-styled bell bottoms. Her face was beautiful but beaten. Her beauty was only befitting the wife of the youngest senior vice president for policy planning in IDC history, but her tired appearance betrayed the fact that she was an alcoholic. She was washing down a librium with a martini, a little concoction she said helped her sleep better now that Blake was so busy with his recent success that he didn't have the energy for other things. But then, of course, he hadn't had the energy for other things for a long time, as she often reminded him.

"I said bullshit. How would you like to be married to the president of IDC?"

"You're kidding," said Teri Corbish.

"Nope," said Blake.

She put an arm on his shoulder and kissed him on the chin, spilling some of her martini on the floor.

"When will this happen?"

"When would you like it to happen?"

"Yesterday," she said, putting her martini on her husband's desk and using the free hand to tickle the buckle on Blake's belt.

"Try within a month."

"Is Broon retiring?"

"In a way."

"You'll be the youngest most powerful executive in America. In the world."

"Yes. It's what I've wanted."

"Then will we be happy?"

Corbish ignored the question. He felt his wife's hand work at his pants zipper.

"Later, Teri. I've work to do. Have another martini."

It took Remo three minutes to realize he had been ordered to eliminate someone. Corbish gave the order personally in his Scarsdale home, apologizing to Remo because he had not introduced his wife, who was upstairs asleep.

"At eight o'clock at night?" asked Remo.

"She's an early sleeper and lately a late riser."

"Oh," said Remo. In all his years in the organization, he had never met Dr. Smith's wife, Maude. He had only once seen that picture of her on Smith's desk. She had the face of frozen biscuit dough. Remo did not see any pictures of Mrs. Corbish in the office or in Corbish's home.

"Our problem," said Corbish, "is that our organization's initial miscalculated thrusts have called for a redeeming support action along similar lines."

"What?"

"As you know, the termination to the extreme of certain IDC employees was wrong."

Remo understood that.

"But now we have the problem of IDC as a corporate counterforce, so to speak."

Remo did not understand that.

"We've created an enemy."

"I got you. Get to the point."

"We're got to eliminate T. L. Broon, president and chairman of the board."

"Sure," said Remo. "Why all the nonsense?"

"I thought you'd like to know."

"I couldn't care less," said Remo. "Are you sure I should be staying at Folcroft? You know Smith was pretty good about this secrecy thing."

"When you reorganize you always centralize."

"Why?"

"Because it gives you great coordinated concentration."

"If you're offering that as an explanation, you've failed. Heard from Smith? Anyone find him yet?"

Corbish's face was somber. No, no one had heard from Smith, and his freedom represented a danger to security. If they could find him, then they could have him institutionalized.

"If the position were reversed," said Remo in a remark he would dearly regret later, "Smith would have you killed."

Corbish registered the statement and expressed his gratitude for administrative help in his new job. But there were more important and dangerous things at hand.

The Broon estate in Darien, Connecticut, was also a shooting range for the Broon family, who were excellent marksmen. While the estate was surrounded by rolling lawns, it was quite deceptive, for the lawns were really open lanes of fire. Broon himself was the 1935 national skeet shooting champion.

"You mean they sit around at home with their rifles?" asked Remo incredulously.

"No, no," said Corbish. "It's a family policy, I guess even a corporate policy, that it should be protected. The old man did this after the big kidnapping flurry when the Lindberg baby was taken."

"So what are you telling me?" asked Remo. At least Smith made himself clear.

"I authorize you to enlist any help you might need."

"Chiun doesn't want to go out tonight," said Remo. "There's something good on television."

"I mean fighting men," said Corbish.

"You mean people to start fights in bars? Why would I need them? I don't understand."

"Military-type help," said Corbish. "The excellent resources at Folcroft have provided us with highly reliable names. We can get them to you in a week and then you can prepare for, let's say, two or three weeks, and then do your job."

Remo screwed his face in bewilderment.

"You want to turn me into a trainer, right?"

"No, no," said Corbish, feeling his temper fray. "I want you to kill T.L. Broon at his Darien estate."

"Good," said Remo, somewhat puzzled. "Tonight?"

"Well, within a few weeks."

"You want me to delay a few weeks. All right," said Remo.

"No. You'll need a few weeks to do this properly. You

82

just can't go up to the Broon estate and luck into some actions like the other day at the sanitarium."

"Oh, you don't think I can do it. I see," said Remo and chuckled.

"Correct," said Corbish, wondering briefly where his wife's librium was. "Now by this Friday, if it isn't too much of a rush. I'd like you to submit your plans to me for your assignment and we'll get input to flex out the approach."

Remo leaned across the desk. "Wouldn't it be a lot easier to just do the thing? How far is Darien from here, thirty miles?"

"Are you mad?" said Corbish. "What if you should fall into his hands? You jeopardize our whole operation. I'm ordering you to bring me something that would indicate a likelihood of success. I know we have the resources and the capability to do this thing. I've seen the results of your work and I know that you must have many people you can call on and a fine equipment profile. I'd like to see it."

"Sure," said Remo. "You'll get the whole thing by morning."

"Good," said Corbish, smiling with great effort. He ushered Remo to the door. Upstairs he heard his wife stirring. She often awoke late in the evening to take another pill and wash it down with another drink. This evening, she would have to fix her own extra martini. He had more work at the office.

He would have to create his own killer arm. His special forces training told him that this man he had to use for a while was unreliable.

Outside in the soft spring night, Remo was unaware that he was unreliable. He didn't have time to be unreliable. He had a job to do.

He stopped briefly at Folcroft to share his strange

experience. Chiun was scribbling something with a goose quill on a piece of thick parchment.

"You know," said Remo, "Smith ended up bananas, but I think this new guy is starting that way."

"All emperors are mad," said Chiun. "They suffer from the illusion of their superiority. Smith was the maddest of all. He was able to hide that illusion by the absence of servants and concubines."

"Funny," said Remo. "I couldn't for the life of me visualize Smith with a concubine."

"That is why even Sinanju couldn't help him. The maddest of all emperors."

"What are you writing?"

"An entry for the journal of Sinanju, explaining to future generations how this master valiantly attempted against massive obstacles to give sense to an emperor in the West, but was rebuffed, and how the master stayed in the land of daily dramas in an attempt to salvage a white pupil who had showed some moderate promise."

"What are you calling it?"

" 'Chiun's Mad Emperor.' "

"So that's where you get your tales of past masters serving in Islamabad and Loniland and Russia."

"Correct. Future generations must know the truth for history in the hands of a man who constantly needs to justify himself becomes like a garment that changes for the needs of the weather. Here I set down truth. Just as I have been taught that Czar Ivan was not terrible, so too will future generations be taught about the mad emperor Smith, lest someone write that he was a good and a competent man and thus tarnish the name of Sinanju."

Remo felt his stomach tighten. "Smitty was okay. It was a tough job."

"It was an easy job if he were sane. But what can one expect from a country discovered only twelve years ago?"

"America was discovered almost five hundred years ago."

"By whom?"

"Christopher Columbus."

"Not by Sinanju. For Sinanju, Chiun discovered America. I wonder if future generations will celebrate my birthday with parades."

"Now that he's gone," said Remo, "I think I liked Smitty. At least I could understand him."

Remo left the sanitarium and rented a car in town and drove to Darien, where just before dawn in the intensity of the last night, he strolled across the wide-open lawns of the Broon estate, past a guard who for a moment thought he saw an even deeper darkness move through the blackness into the Broon mansion.

It was an axiom in his business that lords aways sleep high, so Remo did not bother with the ground floor. With the delicate quiet of a stalking cat, he moved up a large stairway. One did not jar door locks, one froze them with the hands.

In the first large bedroom, Remo paused. An exquisite young woman, with features of marble perfection, slept, a bedlamp lighting her face. Soft brown hair flowed down the large pink pillows, and delicately flowered sheets were thrown aside, revealing breasts rising with the freshness of youth. Ah, thought Remo, business before pleasure. He shut the door.

Remo went down the hall, listening for breathing on the other side of the doors. Actually if one was very still, felt the floor with one's feet, and the body was motionless to a point near death, one could feel the breathing.

At the heavy oaken door one did not need to feel.

The snoring rattled out of it like gravel in a tin garbage can. Remo went inside and saw covers pulled up to a very strong chin. He shut the door behind him and went quietly to the bed.

He shook the man's shoulder.

"T. L. Broon?"

"What?" said Broon coming out of his deep sleep and seeing a figure beside his bed.

"T. L. Broon, something terrible has happened," said Remo. One did not ask a person to identify himself to a stranger when awakened from deep sleep. The reaction might be panic and then denial.

"What's happened?" said Broon, giving Remo all the identification he needed.

"They won't be serving you breakfast in the morning."

"What? What is this? You woke me up to tell me about breakfast? Who the hell are you, sonny?"

"Sorry. Go back to sleep," said Remo, and he put Broon back to sleep so he would no longer snore. Ever.

He looked around the darkened room for some object of Broon's that Corbish might recognize. A briefcase was by the bed. Remo took it.

Outside, the west wing guard thought he saw that deeper darkness again but when he looked at his post's scanner, a new IDC invention for the armed forces, he saw nothing. He would have to get his eyes checked in the morning.

The first person to discover Broon was his valet. He gasped and fainted. The second was the upstairs maid. She shrieked. When his daughter, the chestnut-haired Holly Broon, heard the screaming, she threw a bathrobe over her nude body and ran to her father's room. The valet was ashen-faced, getting to his knees, the maid was shrieking, and no one was attending to her father.

She saw the open mouth, the stillness of his chest. She felt his forehead. Like a slab of liver, she thought.

"He must have had a heart attack," said the valet.

"A heart attack with his temple crushed," said Holly Broon.

"We've already called a doctor," said the valet. "At least someone has."

Holly Broon, who of all the Broons had old Josiah's fierce eyes, ignored the valet's remark. It didn't matter who called the doctors. She phoned the family and corporate lawyers. She had one question.

"Who's next in line at IDC?"

"The picture isn't quite clear on that, Miss Broon. There's got to be a state of mourning first and I'm sure all of us grieve . . ."

"Bullshit. Who's senior vice president for policy planning?"

"Young man, Corbish. Fine outstanding work, a superior . . ."

"Never heard of him. How long's he been senior v.p.?"

"Just a few days, maybe a week, but . . ."

"Give me his telephone number."

The lawyer had it written down somewhere. Holly told a maid to get her something from her wardrobe, in black.

"Something with an open neck. I've got boobs, you know." When she heard the telephone number, she hung up and dialed again.

"Hello, Mr. Corbish. I'm sorry to waken you," said Holly whose voice now floated like doves upon a silken lake. "I have bad news. T. L. Broon passed away last night and while I know you, like all of us, wish a suitable waiting period, the affairs of IDC must continue. I'm Holly Broon and I'd like to meet you as soon as possible.

I think you are the kind of man who can carry on his work."

"Yes, Miss Broon. Of course. Certainly."

"Where can we meet?"

"I have an office just about thirty minutes from you in Rye, New York, on Long Island Sound. It's at Folcroft Sanitarium."

"That's strange," said Holly.

"Well, corporate business. It's a little bit complicated."

"I'm sure you're handling it very well," said Holly and she took directions to Folcroft from her Darien estate.

When her black dress was brought to her, she had one comment.

"More cleavage."

"I don't think you have more cleavage in black, Miss Broon."

"Then fucking make it," said Holly, her voice slate hard. "Use scissors."

"On a St. Laurent dress, Miss Broon?"

"No, on your asshole. Of course, on the dress, knuckle-head."

The estate guards, Holly found out just before she left, had seen nothing the night before. She ran her check on Corbish from the back seat of her limousine. He was a Williams graduate and a special forces captain. He had joined IDC where he had worked steadily, rising rapidly to vice president, and then jumping to senior vice president almost overnight.

"We have more vice presidents than we have computers," Holly said into the telephone in the back of her car. "How did he become someone?"

"Your father appointed him, Miss Broon."

"Is he married?"

"Nine years, Miss Broon."

"The wife attractive?"

"It doesn't say in his personnel record."

"Try the blue file."

"Oh, you know about that."

"Since I could walk."

"Well, I hate to give blue file information over the phone, but I imagine it's important, Miss Broon. Yes, his wife is attractive, but she is a very heavy drinker, takes depressants from time to time, and has had, perhaps, one extramarital affair. She graduated from a somewhat second-rate school in Ohio, her father . . ."

"Has Corbish had any extramarital affairs?"

"No, Miss Broon."

"I see. Keep this conversation to yourself."

"Certainly, Miss Broon."

As she hung up she noticed the chauffeur stealing looks at her bosom. He became embarrassed when he saw that he'd been observed. Good, thought Holly Broon. If you've got it, use it. This Corbish son of a bitch I'm going to fold, spindle and mutilate.

"Did you say something, Miss Broon?" asked the chauffeur.

"I said it's a great tragedy I know you must share with us."

"Yes, Miss Broon."

CHAPTER NINE

When he was informed about T. L. Broon's death, Blake Corbish did not give vent to the shriek of joy that was in his heart. It is the mark of a man who engages in massive spying on other people that even in his own home he behaves as if people were watching him.

With great self-control, Corbish let the receiver sit on the phone cradle a moment, then he nudged his wife, Teri, who had gone to sleep in her sweater and skirt. She had been dozing off like that lately. At first it was a joke, but it had become a habit.

"Dear," said Corbish. "I have good news for you."

"Hmmmmm," said Teri Corbish.

"Open your eyes. I have fantastic news. Good news."

Teri Corbish turned over in bed to face her husband. She felt chilly shakes in her arms and she noticed she had once again succumbed to her habit of sleeping in her clothes.

"You know I waited so long for you to come up that I must have fallen asleep in my clothes again."

"Darling," said Corbish. "T. L. Broon is dead. Just found out. Say hello to the new president of IDC."

"That's fantastic, dear."

"Home free," said Corbish.

"Home free," said his wife. "Let's drink to that. I don't ordinarily drink in the morning but for this, I'm going to."

"President and maybe chairman of the board."

"A double," said Teri.

She stumbled out of bed, then she realized it was not that her feet were unsteady but that a briefcase was in her way on the floor.

"You left your briefcase right in my way."

"It's the martinis, Teri."

"It's the briefcase. Look."

Corbish blinked. Teri was holding T.L.'s briefcase. Was it possible? Yes, it was possible. Williams just might be a fantastic corporate resource. Yet now that he had done his job, he represented a link to tie Corbish to murder.

Corbish steadied himself as he had every morning since taking over the Folcroft operation. Wait. You must have more sock with the courts than the supreme court has, he told himself. You're outside the law. The whole system at Folcroft was set up that way.

Every morning he had constantly had to remind himself of that. In his office at Folcroft, he found himself insulated, strangely free from those worries and this made him wonder why old Dr. Smith had failed to make himself a very, very rich man.

"How did this get in here?" asked Teri.

"Oh, uh, nothing. Just a night delivery, dear."

"The deliveryman could have seen something."

"Between us, Teri?"

"We didn't do it last night?"

"Look at your clothes."

"People do it with their clothes on," she said, then added glumly, "but not us. We don't even do it with our clothes off."

"You've been a fine corporate wife."

"I mean, I'd settle for you right now, instead of the martini."

"Have your martini, dear," said Corbish.

Meanwhile, in a Minneapolis bank, a man who walked with a cane and had portions of his face bandaged, asked to see one of the vice presidents, anyone.

He waited patiently. His clothes hung loosely, like throwaways. His blue shirt had a frayed collar; his shoes, while they had soles and were free of holes, were cracked to submission at the instep. Dr. Harold Smith had picked them up at a Salvation Army chapel on Mission Street in San Francisco. He had hitchhiked across the Rockies, across the Plains states and then north to Minneapolis, where he walked from the small suburb where his ride had let him off to this small bank. Now his right leg throbbed in agony.

"May I ask what your business is about," said the secretary.

"Yes," said Dr. Smith. "A special account."

"You wish to open one?" asked the secretary, trying to hide the suspicion in her voice.

"I have one. Under Densen. William Cudahy Densen. A special account. A savings acount."

"If you want to make a deposit or a withdrawal, the tellers will be glad to help you."

"I want to talk to one of the vice presidents."

"Certainly, sir," said the secretary, in the tone of voice one used to humor infants. She excused herself and went into the most junior vice president's office. She told him about the derelict outside.

92

"What name did you say?"

"William something Densen."

The secretary watched in amazement as the vice president buzzed the president on an intercom.

"Do you remember that funny account you were telling me about, well, someone is here to claim it."

"I'm busy right now," the president said. "Hold him up for a few minutes. I'd like to see him." The vice president nodded and hung up.

"If I may ask, sir, is Mr. Densen someone important?" the secretary asked.

"Oh, no," said the vice president. "It's just that we've had this peculiar account here for the last, oh, eight to ten years. I heard about it when I first came to work here. Somebody deposited some money. I think it was no more than $5,000. He sent it in by mail on American Express travelers' checks. Now you know the law says a person has to show up to open an account. But Densen sent the money with instructions that we should pay anyone with the correct signature. He said it would be all right with the authorities, and no passbook was needed. Well, we naturally reported it to the banking commission, and the commission did say it would be all right."

"And then what?"

"Then nothing. The account just stayed here."

"Drawing interest?"

"No. That's another peculiarity. No interest was asked for. No passbook. No interest. No one showed up. The money just sat."

"Densen certainly does look strange," said the secretary. "Like a bum."

Strange, too, was Densen's request when he received the money. He wanted two hundred dollars in quarters, one hundred dollars in dimes, twenty dollars in nickels, and the rest in twenties and fifties. He carried his money out in a little box. The bank officers watched as he crossed the street to an Army and Navy store. Out of curiosity, the youngest v.p. went to the store to browse. He saw the strange Mr. William Cudahy Densen whose signature had proven valid, buy a bus driver change dispenser, and put it in the box. He saw the strange Mr. Densen go across the street to a clothing store and reemerge in a dull gray suit more than conservative enough for a banker.

Densen's next stop was a stationery store, where he purchased pads, pencils, a slide rule, a billfold and a cheap attaché case.

At the bus station, the young bank officer lost Mr. Densen. He could have sworn he saw him waiting in line. And then there was no one.

Dr. Harold Smith walked out of the Minneapolis bus terminal, mildly amused by the young man's attempt to follow him.

CHAPTER TEN

Of course he would wear a suit, but should it be black? Black might look like instant mourning, and perhaps that was just a shade too obsequious a posture to be adopted by the man who would be the next president of IDC. On the other hand, a light-colored suit might be considered frivolous by Holly Broon in her state of grief over her father's death.

After weighing his options, considering the variables, the upside potential and the downside risks, Blake Corbish decided to wear a black suit with a blue pinstripe. The black covered the mourning, the stripe showed that Corbish was not a man to stand on inane ceremonies, not when the world's greatest corporation was in need of effective leadership. He hoped the point would not be lost on Holly Broon.

He dressed quickly, his mind on T.L.'s daughter and what he knew of her. Indeterminately thirtyish. Pictures in the beautiful people magazines. Inside talk was that she was at least as much the brains of IDC as her father.

Corbish had never met her, but one of the lower-ranking vice presidents had.

He had come into Corbish's office after that meeting six months before. He had wiped sweat from his brow, sighed, lit a cigarette, exhaled the smoke and said, "What a bitch."

Corbish knew whom he meant, but one could never tell what was real or what was a setup, so he asked simply, "Who?"

"That Holly Broon," the other young v.p. had said. "She just cut off my balls and barbecued them."

The vice president had been in charge of a narrow-goaled program to buy up European germanium for use in transistors. It was supposed to be done quietly, but the previous day a line had been dropped into the Wall Street Journal mentioning IDC's interest in European suppliers. This of course had the immediate effect of jamming up the price so that IDC would realize no savings by going overseas.

The idea for the program apparently had been Holly Broon's. The young vice president had met with her that day in T.L.'s Mamaroneck office, in the presence of old T.L. himself.

Corbish remembered thinking that it was odd the young vice president hadn't mentioned T.L. at all. Just Holly Broon. She had impressed him and frightened him. Corbish had listened to the story but he'd said nothing, not wishing to commit himself. Later, he gave his immediate superior hints of the comments made by the young vice president. As he knew it would, the story was passed on to T.L. Soon after, the young vice president was gone.

That was all Corbish knew about her, except of course the pictures he had seen of her. They made her look beautiful. Well, he would wait to see about that. He had seen too many stunning pictures of corporate women who turned out to have all the beauty of footprints, to be impressed by what the camera said.

He glanced at his watch, sneaked a look into his bedroom where Teri had collapsed back onto the bed, her martini spilled on the carpet, its contents darkening the light blue wool. He shook his head and left. There would be time to deal with Teri after he was president of IDC.

When Corbish drove his own Cadillac through the gates, he warned the head guard, "A Miss Broon is coming to see me. Let her right in, then call me."

"Yes sir, Mr. Corbish."

Corbish had his secretary prepare two pots, one of coffee and one of tea, and gave her orders to keep both hot, and to bring them in on a silver service when he buzzed on the intercom.

He buzzed as soon as the guard called him, and by the time Holly Broon swirled into his office, the silver service was sitting on one corner of the conference table. A class touch, Corbish thought, looking at it. A presidential-class touch.

He rose.

"Good morning, Miss Broon, I can't tell you how . . ."

"Then don't try, Corbish," she said. "We've got work to do. She looked at the silver service. "Coffee and tea?"

"Yes. Which would you . . . ?"

"Have any vodka?"

There was, he knew, liquor in one of the cabinets, but now he wondered with some anguish what to do. He had not expected a morning drinker. He did not want to look like a boozer himself by going right to the liquor cabinet. On the other hand, if he delayed getting the drink, it might looked as if he lacked social grace.

He picked up the phone and called his secretary.

"I ordered some liquor the other day for guests. Where is it? Thank you."

He hung up. "It's over here," he said to Holly Broon. "I didn't know where they had put it." There. Social grace and teetotalling in the office.

As he walked to the cabinet, Holly Broon slumped down in one of the large leather chairs facing him across the table. She called out to his back, "A double in a big glass. No ice. No mix."

Another problem. Should he drink with her? Let her drink alone? Oh, the difficulties in drawing the line between corporate image and personal pushiness.

He poured Holly Broon's drink, using a shot glass to measure out exactly two ounces, decided on coffee for himself, but changed his mind at the last minute and poured himself tea. Coffee was so . . . so, plebeian.

Holly had taken her drink from his hand and when he turned toward her with his teacup, her glass was half empty.

"What are you doing here?" she asked.

He had anticipated that question all the way over in his car. And even though Holly Broon now stood to inherit control of ten percent of IDC's outstanding stock, and could guarantee him the corporate presidency, he had decided to tell her as little as he could get away with.

"Before your father's untimely demise," he said, "he put me in charge of a special computer operation. This is where it's headquartered."

How much did she know? Were the stories true about her being old T.L.'s brains? If they were, then she already knew what he was up to. His answer was bland enough to go either way if she gave him any inkling of how much she knew.

He met her eyes straight on, which he knew was the right thing to do, and raised the teacup to his lips so she could not see any telltale expression around his mouth. The eyes can usually disguise a lie, but the mouth rarely can.

"I know you were put in charge. What have you produced?"

"I was working on personal orders from T.L., Miss Broon. It was kind of a novel approach to corporate problems but one with great promise and that showed genius. T.L. wanted a computerized setup of the entire country . . . interrelationships between private industry and government at all levels, the impact of law enforcement, the courts, the unions, yes, even of the criminal element." There. That still gave away nothing.

"Why?" she said. She was making it difficult.

"IDC needed to have solid information on the social structure of the country in order to make sensible long-range decisions based upon our very best planning."

Holly drained the rest of her glass and without a word held it out to Corbish for a refill. As he took the glass from her hand, she said, "You're full of shit."

He turned toward the liquor cabinet before saying, "I beg your pardon."

"I said, you're full of shit. First, T.L., didn't give a rat's ass about social structures. He wanted to sell computers. Second, even if he did, it's hardly likely that he would have bought you this mausoleum to fool around in. Why this place?"

As he refilled the glass, Corbish smiled slightly to himself. "Actually," he said, "this place has been kind of a testing ground for IDC computers for some time. All our latest models are here, even the newest generation that isn't on the market yet. I gather that this place was formerly some kind of government information-gathering network. Much of the information T.L. wanted was already in the computers here, and he sent me up to plug into it for maximum utilization."

He turned with the drink. Holly took the glass and nodded. She held it between the fingertips of both hands and looked over it at Corbish, her head tilted down, her heavy-lashed eyes fixed on him, seductively showing whites under her irises.

Corbish recognized the look and knew he had her. She had given up trying to break him; now she was going to use feminine wiles on him. Why, this would be a piece of cake, he thought.

"How would you like to be the next president of IDC?" she asked.

He lifted then put down his teacup and walked around behind his desk. "I'm overwhelmed, Miss Broon. I never . . ."

"Don't crap me," she said. "You always. All of you vice presidents. And don't think I just promised you anything. I only asked how you'd like to be president."

Blake Corbish, who that morning had considered the power he wielded through CURE, had already decided that he would indeed be president, but not just of IDC. He chose his words carefully and paused before speaking.

"More than anything else I can imagine," he lied.

"You know, as my father's heir, I'm the largest single stockholder."

"Yes, Miss Broon."

"I can't guarantee you anything," she said, "but between my stock holdings and my influence with the board, I think I could pick Mickey Mouse if I wanted."

Corbish nodded. No comment seemed necessary.

"I just wanted to be sure you aren't really Mickey Mouse," she said. "I don't know yet whether you are or whether you just think I am, with that ridiculous story you've been giving me about your work here."

She sipped at her vodka, waiting for a comment. The silence hung in the room for a moment as each cooly took the other's measure. Finally, Corbish said, "You must understand, Miss Broon, that I've been here less than ten days. It would really take more time than that to figure everything out and to draw the kind of conclusions T. L. must have been looking for."

They stared at each other a moment longer, neither satisfied with Blake's no-information answer, and then the telephone rang on Corbish's desk. Without taking his eyes off Holly Broon, he slowly snaked his hand toward it.

In Cleveland, Dr. Harold Smith walked into a telephone booth on a street corner, looked carefully at his newly purchased wristwatch, then dialed the operator.

Ht fished a stopwatch from his jacket pocket as he said, "I'd like to make a long distance call to Rye, New York." He gave the operator the area code and number.

"That will be three dollars and twenty cents," the operator said.

"I'm going to talk for three and a half minutes," Smith said. "How much will the extra minute be?"

"That will be, let's see, seventy cents extra."

"All right, operator. I'll pay for it now. Just a moment please." Smith hooked the receiver on the small shelf under the phone and began to click quarters out of the bus driver's changer he wore on his side under his jacket. He clicked out four, deposited them, did that twice more, then clicked out three more quarters, a dime and a nickel, and put them into the phone.

"Thank you," the operator said, "I'll put the call through now."

Smith heard the beeps on the line as the line transfers were made. He hoped that no one had changed the private line on his desk, which he had used only for outgoing personal calls. Then Smith heard the phone ring. Quickly, he depressed the pushbutton on the stopwatch and looked down at it. The phone was picked up on the first ring.

"Hello," came the voice, sharp, crisply efficient as Smith had remembered it, with little accent and no trace of regionalism.

Smith waited a few seconds until the voice said "hello" again.

"Corbish," Smith asked.

"Yes."

"This is Smith." Smith glanced at his watch. Twenty seconds had gone by. He heard a sudden sip of air at the other end of the phone and then a quick recovery.

"Well, hello, doctor, where are you?"

"That's really rather immaterial," said Smith drily. "You've installed yourself at Folcroft, I take it?"

"Why not? Someone has to keep things running."

"I've called, Corbish, to appeal to you." By now, Smith figured, Corbish should have recovered from the shock of Smith's voice and should be reaching for the switch that would activate CURE's elaborate phone-tracing system.

"What kind of appeal?" came Corbish's voice. Right, Smith thought. Ask questions. Keep the old fool talking.

"I wanted to appeal to you to give up this mad enterprise you're conducting."

"I don't know why you should consider it mad, doctor. It's very sensible, that is, from a corporate point of view. Don't you agree."

"No, I don't agree," Smith said. "But if I can't talk to you from that standpoint, perhaps as an American. Can't

102

you see you're tampering with the very structure of our society? That there could be dangerous ramifications of what you are doing?"

"There is no gain without pain," Corbish said. "Personally, I think the gain will be worth the effort. Can you imagine the power I will have?"

They talked on. Smith asked questions, Corbish countered and asked his own questions.

When his stopwatch hit the three-minute mark, Smith said, "Never mind then, Corbish. I just wanted to warn you of something."

"Oh. What's that?"

"I'm going to kill you."

Corbish laughed. "I'm afraid you've got it wrong, Doctor Smith. You're not going to kill me."

The stopwatch's second hand passed twenty.

"Well, we'll just have to see about that," Smith said. "By the way, have you met Remo?"

"Yes."

"Don't think he'll do a job on me for you," Smith said. "He's too loyal to me for that."

Corbish laughed again. "Loyal?" he said. "He doesn't even remember your name."

He started to say more but was unable to. The sweep secondhand of the stopwatch was nearing the minute and Smith hung up the telephone.

He stepped out of the telephone booth and looked around. His face caught the eyes of an old man inside a tailor shop on the street next to the booth. Smith locked eyes with the man a moment, then stepped down the stairway leading to the city's subway system. He stopped at the change booth and bought one token, careful to pay with loose coins from his outside jacket pocket.

"When is the next train uptown?" he asked.

103

The bored token seller said, "Every five minutes, Mister."

"What track?" Smith said.

"Over there," said the token seller, looking up in annoyance, which was what Smith wanted him to do.

"Thank you," Smith said.

He took the token and used it to get through the turnstile leading to the uptown train platform. He walked casually along the platform, trying not to draw attention to himself. At the far end of the platform, he moved through an exit turnstile, headed for the flight of stairs that he knew was nearby and went back up to street level.

He came out of a subway kiosk diagonally across the street from the phone booth, and slid behind the wheel of a parked, unlocked car which he had left there several hours before.

He slumped down in the seat and pulled his hat down slightly over his eyes. He glanced at his watch. It should be any moment now.

Tracing a dialed call within the city limits generally took CURE's elaborate electronic network seven minutes. But an out-of-town call handled by an operator took only three minutes and twenty seconds to trace. Smith had given Corbish enough time. Now to wait and see how much control Corbish had over CURE's operations in the field.

Smith lighted a cigarette. Although he hated the taste and considered smoking a vile habit, he had found that nicotine was a reasonably effective pain duller. Now, he clung to the habit, even though the pain had lessened and he was able to walk, using his right leg almost normally.

Midway in his third drag, an unmarked tan Chevrolet sedan pulled up to the phone booth. Two men in light

104

gray suits stepped out and looked both ways down the street. One of them went into the phone booth and Smith could see him examine the floor and the shelf under the phone.

Smith's stomach sank involuntarily. FBI. The two men wore their anonymity like public address systems. The first man came out of the booth and moved toward the dry cleaning store, while the second agent continued to look both ways along the street.

After only a minute, the first agent came out of the store, motioned to his partner, and they started down the steps toward the subway station.

Smith waited until both of them were out of sight before he started the motor of the car he had purchased that morning. He drove across the intersection and down two blocks before turning right and heading downtown.

Smith doubted that the agents would be taken in by his dodge in asking for the uptown schedule. But that didn't matter. In a few minutes he would be on his way out of the city.

What did matter was that Corbish knew how to work the phone-tracing systems and even more important, he knew how to move the vast federal apparatus into action. It had been no more than eight minutes from the time Smith hung up until the two agents appeared.

As he drove mechanically along, Smith realized how Dr. Frankenstein must have felt when his creation ran amok.

Corbish had CURE; he knew how to make it work, and if his conversation was accurate—and why shouldn't it be?—he had Remo, too. And Smith had, he reflected wryly, something less than four thousand dollars, a bus driver's change maker, a stopwatch and a slide rule.

Maybe it was enough.

CHAPTER ELEVEN

After hanging up on Smith, Corbish had a problem. If he waited to get Holly Broon out of the office, he would lose any chance he had to get Smith. But if he started the apparatus in motion, she would suspect something was up, if she did not indeed already suspect.

Smith was more important right now. Corbish picked up the phone and dialed a three-digit number.

"There's a trace on a phone call which just came into this office. Get it and have some men try to locate the man who made the call. Yes, that's right. Find and detain the man. I'll handle it personally. Advise me of results." He hung up without waiting for a response, then he looked up at Holly Broon.

"Now where were we?" he said mildly.

"Where we were," she said, "was that I was advising you to stop shitting me. And now, after this phone call business, I think it's best that you level with me right away."

The tone of her voice made her seriousness clear, and

because Blake Corbish did not yet have the presidency of IDC locked up, he decided to talk to her.

"All right, Miss Broon, I'll explain. But first let me say that while he was alive your father gave me specific instructions not to mention this to anyone. He specifically included you, and I think he feared for your safety. I was just following orders."

This man is lying to me, Holly Broon thought, but she only nodded.

"What we have in here, Miss Broon, is control of a secret agency of the United States government. It's not just information gathering. It includes a pipeline into every functioning arm of the government, the FBI, the IRS, the CIA. With this agency in our control, IDC can do virtually anything it wants. There's no politician we can't reach, nothing we can't do."

He smiled and Holly Broon realized it was his first real smile since she had entered the room.

"What's this agency called?"

"Its name is CURE, but I'm sure you've never heard of it. That's the entire point of it. No one's heard of it, except a small handful of people. Those people outside, the guard on the gate, the computer staffers, none of them know who they're working for. That's the beautiful part."

"And that phone call?"

"That, unfortunately, was one of the people who has heard of it," Corbish said. "The former director. I'm trying to track him down now. He's probably dangerous."

"And if you do 'track him down,' as you put it?"

"I'll continue to carry out your father's instructions, Miss Broon. I won't let him stand in our way."

He's mad, Holly Broon thought. But still, the idea was intriguing. If IDC controlled the country, it could control

107

the world. Josiah, the Broon she most resembled in character, would have understood.

She grilled Corbish for another hour, consuming two more vodkas in the process. He answered truthfully, telling her about everything except the true function of Remo and Chiun. Thoughtfully, he had decided that might be just too tantalizing; she might want to meet them; she might suspect that Remo had killed Broon, and from there it would be an easy jump to conclude it had been done on Corbish's orders.

Finally, Holly Broon had had enough. The phone rang again. Corbish answered it with a breezy "hello," then he listened. When he hung up, his face was sour. "Dr. Smith got away," he said.

"Now what?"

"I'll figure out something."

"You won't have heard the last of him," she said. "He's going to come after you. He'll leave tracks. Keep your eyes open for his tracks."

"Thank you, I will."

Holly Broon stood up. She moved around the back of Corbish's desk. He had not yet examined her cleavage and that disturbed her slightly.

She leaned over the corner of his desk, toward him, so that the cleavage was unmistakable and unignorable. She had to give him credit; he tried to ignore it.

"I'm going to like working with you, together," she said, stretching out the "together" to emphasize its togetherness. "We can make some kind of magic here."

He smiled at her, and met her eyes, happy at the opportunity to stop looking at her bosom.

"I think you're right," he said.

"Congratulations on your impending elevation to the presidency of IDC."

"Thank you, Miss Broon. I really am sorry about your father."

"Call me Holly. And let's do ourselves a favor. Let's not crap each other. My father was a thick-headed bastard who inherited a corporation and wasn't quite dumb enough to ruin it. In fact, what I can't figure out is how he had enough sense to send you after CURE."

Corbish looked at her, searching her eyes. "Frankly," he said, "neither could I."

Both smiled. "We understand each other now," she said. "One more question?"

"Yes?"

"Why is your wife an alcoholic?"

"She can't take corporate pressure. I think she expected me to be a pipe and slippers type."

"A man on the rise like you may need a more compatible helpmate," Holly Broon said.

"You may be right."

She stood up straight. "I'll have my father's funeral in three days. In the meantime, IDC'll roll along by itself. If any decisions are needed, you and I will make them. I'll call a meeting of the executive committee after the funeral, and we'll name you president. Anything wrong with that schedule?"

"No, Miss Broon . . . Holly."

"I'll talk to you tomorrow."

On the way back to her car, Holly Broon mused about how the structure of large corporations seemed to protect them from all kinds of managerial abuse. Her father had been a fool who had to be dragged kicking and screaming into the twentieth century. Blake Corbish was younger, perhaps a little smoother, but not really any brighter. He thought the use of CURE would end with IDC's super-success. He had no greater ambitions. It was unfortunate, she thought, that his vision was so limited. With CURE in his pocket, a person could take over the world.

Check that, she thought. With CURE in *her* pocket, a woman could take over the world.

First she would have to take over Blake Corbish. The world was next.

Still she would have felt better if he had been more interested in her cleavage.

CHAPTER TWELVE

Holly Broon had misjudged Blake Corbish. Despite his deficiencies as a boob-man, he had no shortage of vision. One of his secrets was that he was singlemindedly ambitious without giving the impression of being over-ambitious and, therefore, dangerous. It explained the corporate corpses of a number of vice presidents that Blake Corbish had clambered over on his way to the top. The final corporate corpse was just that—a corpse—and Blake Corbish would soon be on the top of the heap. At least the top of the IDC heap.

There were other heaps to climb: the United States, the world.

Corbish now had no doubt about his ability to handle Holly Broon. Her clumsy pass at him was not much less than a proposal of marriage. It probably would be a good idea, too, solidifying his control of IDC through stock ownership, and it might solve the problem of his drunken wife.

Still, there was divorce to consider. The American people had grown more sophisticated, but were they ready yet to elect a divorced man as President of the United States?

Blake Corbish looked at the straight pen in the old-fashioned inkwell on his desk, which he had selected as a someday-publicizable idiosyncracy, and he pondered for a moment.

Divorce? Then he broke up laughing. Why divorce?

Why divorce when an accident would suffice? And he had at his control the world's finest lethal accident creator. Remo Williams. He stopped laughing abruptly and reached for the phone. But there were other things for Remo to do first.

"The first thing you've got to do," Corbish told Remo officiously, "is to find Smith."

"Just find him?" Remo asked.

"For the time being, just find him," Corbish said.

"That's not really in my field of strengths, activity-wise, corporately speaking," Remo said. "I'm more a doer than a looker."

"No one knows Smith better than you," Corbish said. "I thought you might have the best chance of tracking him down."

Remo shrugged, a small gesture of displeasure.

"Of course," Corbish said, "this problem would not have arisen if you had disposed of the Smith question when you first saw it coming up."

"All right, all right," Remo said. This eternal bitching was getting on his nerves.

"He called from Cleveland," Corbish said. "Ohio."

"I'm glad you straightened that out for me," Remo said. "I was thinking of Cleveland, Alabama."

"How will you proceed?" Corbish asked.

"I don't know. I told you I'm not much of a looker. I thought I might put an ad in the *Cleveland Plain Dealer*. Tell Smith to turn himself in right away or have his credit cards revoked. How would I know how I'm going to proceed? I don't even know where he is, for God's sake. I can tell you one thing; he's not waiting for us in Cleveland."

"Where would he be likely to turn up?"

"The Ladies Sodality of the First United Wasp Church would be my guess," Remo said. "You know this room hasn't changed much at all since I was first here? That was, oh, ten years ago."

"Yes, yes," Corbish said impatiently. "Well, do what you think is best. Just get Smith. Are you taking the Chinaman with you?"

"The Chinaman? You mean Chiun?"

Corbish nodded.

"Do us all a favor," Remo said. "I don't want to have to deal with still another director. Don't ever call him a Chinaman to his face. Chiun is Korean."

"So?" Corbish said, demonstrating in one word his belief that Korean, Chinese, Japanese, it was all the same to him.

"Don't ever say it," Remo said.

"All right. By the way, that was a good performance on the T. L. Broon assignment."

"Thanks," said Remo, warming to the kind of praise he had never been able to draw from Smith.

"Well, that will be all," Corbish said. He reached into his desk drawer and pulled out a plastic tag. "By the way," he said, handing the tag to Remo, "you might start wearing this. It will facilitate your entrance into the grounds."

Remo looked at the playing card-sized pieces of plastic embossed with his name and a long serial number. "You mean I should shlepp this around?"

"No. It has a pin on the back. Wear it."

113

"It seems kind of strange, considering the work I do and all."

"Leave the policy quanta to me. Do as you're told. And find Smith."

Remo left the office. Outside the room, he shredded the plastic tag in the palm of his right hand, and dropped it into a wastepaper basket. When he went outside, he scaled the twelve-foot high stone wall, and to cool off his anger, ran all the way into town and rented the first motel room he could find.

Later, in the room, he confided to Chiun, "I don't think this new guy is playing with a full deck."

"Aha, you see. Already Chiun's words are coming true. You now dislike your new emperor."

"I didn't say I dislike him. But can you imagine giving me an identification tag?"

"It is often done with children. So they do not get lost on buses," Chiun said.

"Come on. You're going to love Cleveland."

"Cleveland? Why are we going to Cleveland? What is in Cleveland?"

"Smith was seen there."

"And of course he is still there waiting for you?"

"Maybe not, but maybe we can pick up his tracks."

Chiun shook his head sadly. "I think you and your Mr. Garbage have confused the mad emperor Smith with a rabbit. He will not leave any tracks."

"Orders are orders," Remo said. "That's the way Corbish wants it."

"Well, then, by all means, we must run. Mr. Garbage has issued an order. Let us not question it; let us take leave of our senses too, and go running off to Cleveland, wherever that is, to look for a man that we know has left Cleveland. Very clever, your new emperor."

"Can the chatter. We've got to look for Smith."

114

In a motel room outside Cincinnati, Smith waited; he expected that Remo would soon be after him.

It had been a risk he had to take, calling Corbish, but he had to find out how much the man knew and how much control he had of CURE. The prospect of having Remo after him had taken second place in Smith's mind, but now he could think about it.

The issue wasn't even Smith's life. In his patrician view of things, that was perhaps the least important thing. The country was the most important. With Corbish at the controls of CURE, the entire country lay open to him like a fresh fruit pie. He could cut whatever size slices he wanted.

Eventually, the President would realize that CURE was not working correctly. Perhaps the President might even turn the money off. But by that time—if that time ever came, if the President himself had been able to stay free of Corbish's control—by that time, the damage would have been done.

Smith had thought about all this while driving out of Cleveland, his injured right leg throbbing with pain, forced nevertheless to stay steady on the gas pedal, keeping the car moving along at one mile under the speed limit.

Three times he stopped at roadside gas stations with phone booths situated far from the gas station offices. Using his change counter, he had placed three calls to the White House, trying to contact the President. How different it was from his office. There, Smith merely picked up the telephone inside his right desk drawer. It rang in the President's bedroom. No one else dared answer that phone.

But calling the White House through the switchboard to talk to the President was like trying to shave one whisker at a time.

The first time, he got nowhere.

The second time, he got an administrative assistant who seemed annoyed that an American should attempt to get a phone call through to the headquarters of America's government.

"Your name is what, sir?" the assistant had asked with artificial politeness.

"My name is Dr. Smith. What is yours?"

"Fred Finlayson. I'm an administrative assistant to the President."

"Well, Mr. Finlayson," said Smith, "this is very important. A matter of extreme urgency to the country." Even as he said it, Smith realized he must sound like one of the hundreds of hooples who called the White House every day to warn the President of the impending fluoridation disaster, the Red Menace in comic books and how pornography was destroying the minds of even unconsenting adults.

"I know I probably sound like a crackpot," Smith said, "but it is imperative that the President be told that I called. And no one else must be told. Mr. Finlayson, you will guarantee your successful future in government if you do this thing. It is now 1:45 P.M. your time. I will call again at three P.M. If you have given my message to the President, he will wish to speak with me. I will ask for you when I call again."

"Right, sir. Leave it with me."

"Do you have my name?"

"Better give it to me again, sir."

"Doctor Harold Smith. The President will recognize it, even though you do not."

"Sure thing, Doctor Smith. I'll get right on it."

But even as he hung up, Smith knew that Finlayson would not. The assistant probably had never spoken to the President since he had worked at the White House;

it was hardly likely that he was now going to barge into the Oval Office and let the President know about the interesting crank call he had received that day.

Nevertheless, Smith called back 75 minutes later from another wayside phone booth. He had stood for 10 minutes, waiting for his watch to reach the hour mark.

He asked the White House switchboard for Fred Finlayson, and after a long series of buzzes, the amused young voice of a woman answered, "Mr. Finlayson's office."

"This is Doctor Smith. Is Mr. Finlayson in?"

He could hear muffled voices off the telephone. Then he could heard laughter and a voice saying, "he's got a loose upper plate." Hardly able to restrain outright laughter, the girl came back on the phone and said, "I'm sorry, Doctor Smith. I've just checked and Mr. Finlayson has gone home for the day."

"He left no message for me?"

"No, sir, I'm sorry."

"When you see Mr. Finlayson again, perhaps just by turning around, tell him that I strongly suggest he begin reading the Help Wanted colums of the local press."

Rather than hear another laugh, Smith hung up. He waited a few moments in the phone booth, shaking his head sadly. If Albert Einstein had tried to use a telephone to warn President Roosevelt about the danger of the Nazis developing an atomic bomb, the world would now be speaking German. Fortunately, Einstein had written.

But that was out of the question for Smith, and so obviously was trying to reach the President by phone.

It had been a stupid attempt and it had created a new problem. No doubt, Smith's name would now be on the confidential reports that flowed out of the White House every four hours to wind up in CURE's computers,

Corbish would without doubt see the name, and when the phone calls were tracked down, it would outline Smith's route as clearly as if he had sent Corbish a road map.

So Smith got into his car, veered off at the next major intersection, and hours later pulled into a motel room outside Cincinnati, where he paid cash in advance.

Smith lay on the motel bed, thinking.

Remo might be his hope. Remo could remove Corbish from CURE. Or, he could get into the White House to have the President confirm that Smith was still the head of CURE and that Corbish was an impostor.

But if he just sought Remo out, it was possible that Remo might have been taken in by Corbish enough to kill Smith on the spot. It was what he had been trained to do.

Smith had to arrange to meet Remo on neutral ground, where Smith would have some control of the outcome. He thought about that for a long time as he smoked, trying to forget the rising pain in his right leg.

Then he sat up and reached for the telephone.

CHAPTER THIRTEEN

"All right, Chiun," Remo demanded. "You look at this and tell me *my* emperor is cracked."

In his hand, Remo held a telegram and he waved the yellow paper in front of Chiun's face.

Chiun ignored him. He sat on the floor in the middle of their Cleveland hotel room, studiously and laboriously scratching one letter at a time on his long parchment scroll. He paid no more attention to the telegram than if it had been a microbe.

Remo kept waving it.

"Read it to me," Chiun said.

"Okay," Remo said. "Okay. Okay. Okay. You want to hear it, I'll read it to you. Are you ready for this?"

"I won't know until you read it. If you ever do," Chiun said, putting down his goose quill. "Since you must speak aloud, you are permitted to move your lips when you read."

"Right," Remo said. "Right. Right. Here's what it says. It says: 'Remo. When are you going to hit a homerun?'

And it's signed H. S. That's Smith. Now what do you think of that?"

"I think we are fools to be in Cleveland because Emperor Smith is not here. I think anyone who sent us to Cleveland is a fool also. And I think the only one besides me, who is not a fool, present company included, is Smith himself."

Remo crumpled the telegram in his hand and dropped it on the floor.

"So that's what you think?"

"Precisely," Chiun said. "Do you wish to take notes? Shall I repeat it?"

"No. Once was enough. More than enough. You've changed your mind already? Now you don't think Smith is mad?"

"I have always thought that Smith was mad. But he is not a fool."

Remo was about to pursue Chiun's statement when the telephone rang. It was Corbish.

"Well?" he asked.

"Well what?"

"Did you find him?"

"No," Remo said. "But he found us. He sent us a telegram. Do you want me to sing it to you?"

"What kind of voice do you have?"

"Very funny," Remo said.

"This is important," Corbish said. "We've learned that Smith called the White House twice. From pay phones on the road from Cleveland to Dayton. I suggest you look for him in Dayton."

"I suggest you look for him in your hat," Remo said. "Do you think he went to Dayton after leaving you a map of telephone calls?"

"Perhaps. Remember, he's crazy."

"He's got plenty of company. Anyway, I know he's not in Dayton. He sent us the telegram from Cincinnati."

"Well then, go there, man. What are you waiting for?"

"For a true twentieth century renaissance," said Remo.

"Get with it," Corbish said. "And no more failures." He hung up.

Remo looked at the phone, then pulled the wire out of the wall. He turned to see Chiun had resumed writing his history of the mad Emperor Smith.

"All right, Chiun, where would you look for Smith?"

"I would not look for him."

"But if you had to?"

"I would let him find me. I would return home."

Remo looked blank.

Chiun looked disgusted. Finally, he said, "Come, we shall look for Doctor Smith in Alaska. I hear the weather there is wonderful this time of year. Or perhaps Buenos Aires or London. Let us run, run, run. There are only three billion people in the world. We may bump into him in a telephone booth somewhere."

"All right. Enough's enough."

"Are we returning to New York?"

"No. We're going to Cincinnati where the telegram came from."

"Wonderful," Chiun said. "A stroke of genius. Your brilliant new employer, Mr. Garbage, will be very proud of you."

"Corbish, Chiun, not garbage."

"They are indistinguishable."

Smith had long since left his motel room outside Cincinnati. He had spent the better part of the day in a small public library reading back issues of the *New York Times*, and he had just learned of the death of T. L. Broon.

With a sinking feeling in the pit of his stomach, Smith had read the news accounts. He realized that Remo was indeed working for Corbish. The death of T. L. Broon had Remo's stamp on it. Anonymity, efficiency, speed. And it had been covered up by the family as death by natural causes.

The paper also mentioned Corbish as a possible successor; they said the major responsibility for the decision would rest with Holly Broon, T. L. Broon's daughter and heir, who was now the world's single biggest stockholder of IDC. That gave Smith something to think about. There might be some gain to be made there.

CHAPTER FOURTEEN

Blake Corbish ignored the heavy breathing of his wife, slipped from the bed, showered, shaved, dressed and quickly left his house for the almost-hurried drive to Folcroft Sanitarium.

He had taken to spending almost all his waking hours at the CURE headquarters, fascinated by the depth of the information in the agency's computers, revelling in the knowledge of what he could do with it.

He drove through the gates at Folcroft, nodding patronizingly to the guard who gave him a semiformal military salute as he entered. One day, he would have flags on the front fenders of his car, and that guard might not be just a civilian guard, but a soldier, a detachment of soldiers, and the salute might not be half-hearted but the kind of crisp formal greeting that soldiers are taught to give their commander in chief.

That day might not be far off. Tomorrow, T. L. Broon would be buried. The next day, Corbish would become president of IDC. It was not too soon to begin planning his campaign for the presidency of the United States.

He had not yet made up his mind whether he would run as a Democrat or a Republican. While he had voted in every general election since becoming twenty-one—all IDC executives voted—he had never declared his party affiliation by voting in a primary. He would make that decision when he saw which party's leadership was more susceptible to his special brand of persuasion.

He sat at his desk with his jacket still on, his tie still pulled tight; the only concession he made to the pressure of worktime was that he opened the front buttons of his jacket.

On paper, he began to plan a program that would produce reports on the Republican and Democratic party chairmen in all fifty states. It would be interesting to find out just what these loyal defenders of the faith and the American Process had been involved in over the last few years. Interesting and perhaps profitable. It would certainly be a strong bargaining point for Corbish when he began to travel the country, seeking support for his presidential ambitions.

Republican or Democrat?

Why worry? Blake finally decided. Perhaps, just perhaps, he might run as the unity candidate of both parties, a man nominated by acclamation, a man chosen by both groups as *the man* to lead the nation out of these dangerous times, a man who would be more than a President of the United States, a man who would be almost an emperor.

It took Corbish ninety minutes to work out the program he needed to pull just the correct information out of CURE's massive memory banks. He could have had someone draw the program for him, but he wanted no one to know what information he sought, and he liked to keep his hand in.

After completing the program, Corbish pushed himself

back from his desk, wheeled the chair around and looked out at Long Island Sound.

There were some problems still to resolve along his inexorable march to the Presidency. The first of them was Smith. He must be found and eliminated. He was, without doubt, powerless now, or else he would not have tried something so foolish as calling the White House. Still, there was a chance he might get lucky. Always a chance that he might get to someone somewhere who could untangle CURE's apparatus and bring it crashing down on Corbish's head.

Corbish too was beginning to doubt if Remo alone were the man to find Smith. He didn't seem to have quite the organizational mind for that kind of work.

It was even possible, Corbish mused, looking out at the waves eating up small pieces of the shoreline, that Smith had made a mistake in the selection of Remo. The job he had done on T. L. Broon might have just been good luck. Remo was, more than likely, just a soldierly CIA-type without much imagination, someone who would rather talk than do.

When this was resolved, Corbish would have to deal with him. Either dispose of him quietly or else give him some other kind of job which would guarantee his loyalty and keep him quiet. Perhaps Remo would like to be head of security at Folcroft. He might like wearing a uniform and playing general.

But that was the future. Now was now, and the problem was Smith.

Blake reached for the telephone, dialed a string of numbers, and then began talking to a man in Pittsburgh who had often done special work for IDC—special work that it was best that law enforcement agencies not find out about.

"Yes, his name is Smith," Corbish said. He gave a

physical description of CURE's former director. "He has been seen in Cleveland and Cincinnati and he is, I'm sure, heading east, obviously by car."

He paused a moment as he saw a memo on his desk that he had overlooked earlier. "Just a second." He read the memo, smiled, and returned to the telephone.

"We've learned that he bought a car in Cleveland under the name of William Martin. License plate Ohio 344-W-12. Yes. He has to be taken care of. I don't care how many men it takes. Get it done. The man who does it will never have to work again."

In a motel room ten miles outside Pittsburgh, Dr. Harold W. Smith woke up, as he did almost everything else, in military fashion. One moment he was asleep. The next moment he was wide awake, his brain whirring, moving as alertly as if he had been awake and at work for hours.

It was one of the things he had learned in wartime spy service. There was danger in lying in bed, luxuriantly half-awake and half-asleep, unconscious to the stirrings of the outside world. A spy learned to sleep light and wake instantly. Smith had never forgotten the lessons.

Today would be a critical day. The telegram to Remo would no doubt have confused him. It would take him time to figure out what Smith had meant.

In the meantime, Smith would see what he could do about confusing Blake Corbish's life.

He would also have to get rid of his car today. By now, they had probably tracked down the man from whom he had bought it, even though Smith had been careful to buy it from a private owner and not from a car dealer. The car had to be changed. If he had been functioning better, he would have done it yesterday, Smith thought.

His right leg still hurt, but less than it had, and he noticed clinically that his limp was less pronounced. Still he showered leaning against the wall of the shower and putting most of his weight on his left leg. He dressed in his gray suit, then he carefully refilled his change maker from the rolls in his attaché case.

It might also be a good idea to procure a weapon today. One never knew, Smith thought, as he hooked the change maker onto his belt under his jacket, took a long look around the room to make sure he had not forgotten to do anything or left anything behind, and then walked toward the door.

Personal preference plus a face that looked as if it were the archtypal leprechaun had combined to cause Pasquale Riotti to carry the nickname Patsy Moriarty.

He found it handy. Police were much less likely to hassel someone named Moriarty.

However he did not like being called Patsy Moriarty on the telephone at eight A.M. when he was just waking up and getting a good daylight look at the blonde chippie lying in bed next to him.

He did not remember his passions of the night before or indeed whether he had even had any. But a look at the blonde's naked body was enough to stir his passions in the morning. He was about to indulge those passions when the telephone rang on the bedstand in his efficiency apartment located in a Pittsburgh suburb.

Patsy Moriarty swore. He watched the blonde stir in response to the telephone's noise, then he lifted the receiver.

"Hello," he growled. He didn't like being bothered when he was busy.

But Patsy Moriarty didn't mind being called at any time by the voice on the other end of the phone. It was a man by whose sufferance Patsy lived and at whose direction Patsy had made sure a lot of other people no longer lived.

Moriarty sat up straight in bed. "Yes sir," he said. And then he listened. He kept a pad and pencil next to the bed and now he used it to take notes.

"Yes, sir," he said. "I have it. I'll get on it right away. Just curious, sir, is there a price? I see. Your personal guarantee is good enough for anybody, sir."

The blonde was awake by the time Patsy hung up and she reached a tentative hand around his body and placed it on top of his bare right thigh.

"Get your clothes on and beat it," Moriarty said.

She looked hurt, but Patsy, whose back was to her, could not see her face. All he could see was her hand and she had not removed it. He reached down with his right hand, grabbed the flesh alongside her thumb and squeezed.

"Owwww," she cried.

"I said, get out of here. I got work to do, so make it fast."

The hand pulled away as if Patsy's thigh had been a hot stove. The blonde scrambled out of bed and began to hurriedly put on her few items of clothing.

Moriarty looked at her naked body.

"Tell me," he asked, "we make it last night?"

"I don't remember," she said. "I was too drunk."

The answer annoyed Moriarty. The least she could have done was remember.

"G'wan, get out of here," he said. "I'll call you sometime."

The blonde, accustomed to years of hasty retreats, was dressed and gone in little more than a minute.

By that time, Patsy Moriarty had figured his course of action. There would be absolutely no point in driving aimlessly around the area, trying to find somebody named William Martin.

The telephone was the answer. He took the phone book from the bedstand drawer and with dismay looked down the column after column of motels and hotels. It would take forever by himself.

Moriarty reached for a well-worn personal phone book and began calling people who owed him.

To each of them, he said the same thing. Check motels and hotels. Look for a guy named William Martin. Driving a tan Dodge, Ohio license 344-W-12. He may be using a fake name. Find out where he is, what room, and get back to me. If you find him, tell the motel guy to keep his mouth shut and you'll duke him later. Now get on it.

It took eighteen phone calls for Moriarty to assure himself that he had covered Pittsburgh and its suburbs thoroughly. Then there was nothing to do but wait. Instead of showering, he washed at the sink to make sure he could get to the phone quickly if it rang. Sure enough, it rang just as he was putting shaving cream on his face.

"Yeah," he said into the phone. Then he listened, taking notes. "Right. Happy Haven Motel. Twenty miles outside the city. Yeah, I know where it is. He's using the name of Fred Finlayson. Okay. You're sure the license plates check? Right. Good. I'll take care of you later on."

Twenty-five minutes later, Patsy Moriarty was parking his Cadillac in the lot of the Happy Haven Motel, across the way from the target's room.

He expected no trouble. The tan Dodge was still parked in front of Room 116. That meant Finlayson or Martin or whatever his name was was still inside.

Moriarty would just wait him out, for the rest of the

day and tomorrow if necessary, because there was one thing he knew. No one could stay too long inside one room. Sooner or later, he'd have to step out and get some air. That was always the problem with Mafia men when they hit the mattresses and went into hiding. The opposition just waited for them to get bored, and then they picked them off as they came out.

Staying cooped up would be even tougher for someone who wasn't used to it, and this guy wasn't. What was it Patsy had been told? He was some kind of a doctor, and he was threatening important people? And he was screwy to boot. Well, whatever it was, it didn't matter, because Moriarty knew all that he needed to know about him. First, that the man must be killed, second, where the man was, and third, that Patsy would be paid for the job.

So he would just sit there and wait for the man to come out of the room and when he did, Patsy would casually get out of his car, walk up to him, and shoot him in the head. No problems at all.

Inside Room 116, Dr. Harold Smith looked around the room. He had not forgotten anything. He walked toward the door, but before opening it, he reached for the pull cord to open the drapes and let the maid know the room was empty and could be cleaned.

But, as befitted an eight-dollar-a-night motel, the pull string did not work and Smith walked to the center of the drapes to pull them apart by hand.

He put his hands on each of the pair of drapes, started to pull, but when the drapes had opened only an inch, he saw the black Cadillac with the man sitting behind the wheel parked across the lot. Smith released the drapes. They stayed a half-inch apart and through the opening he watched the car. It took him fifteen minutes of waiting and watching to be sure. The man was interested only in Smith's car and Smith's room. He fiddled with something in his lap, which was more than likely a pistol.

Smith retreated into the room and picked up the telephone.

When the clerk answered, Smith said, "This is Mr. Finlayson in Room 116. Has anyone been calling for me today?"

The pause before the "no" told Smith that someone had indeed been looking for him. It was the car; they had tracked it down.

"Fine," Smith said. "I want you to send over a boy with a laundry cart. Right away. Yes, of course, to my room. And I'll be staying another day. Thank you."

Smith hung up and raised the back of his right hand to his forehead.

He was sweating, he realized. He could not remember having perspired under pressure since the final days of World War II, when he had been captured briefly by the Nazis. They had gotten the ridiculous idea that he was involved somehow with the American OSS, before the American businessman had been able to set them straight.

Smith returned to the window and kept watch on the Cadillac and its occupant to make sure he got no messages from anyone. The man was still sitting at the wheel of the car when there was a knock on the door a moment later.

"Who is it?" Smith called.

"Bellhop," came a young voice.

Smith opened the door slowly. It was a teenage boy, wearing jeans and a white sweatshirt and dragging behind him one of the large rectangular canvas laundry carts that motels used.

Smith moved to the side to get out of the line of sight

of the man in the Cadillac, pulled the door open, and said "Bring that cart right in here. Hurry up."

The boy moved into the room, pulling the cart, and Smith quickly closed the door.

In the Cadillac across the lot, Patsy Moriarty watched the activity, shrugged and relaxed. Just taking sheets off the bed. Standard procedure for a motel.

He decided to wait.

Inside the room, Smith opened his attaché case on the bed and turned to the confused youth.

He took a twenty-dollar bill from the case, closed the case, and handed the bill to the boy. "This is what I want you to do for that twenty dollars," he said. "Now listen very carefully."

It made Smith uneasy to have to put his faith in a young man about whom he knew nothing, but without a weapon, he had no alternative, and desperate situations called for desperate measures.

Across the lot, Moriarty continued to watch the door of the room. The kid was taking long enough to strip the beds, he thought.

The door opened and the laundry cart appeared, the boy pushing it from behind. Outside the door, the kid turned, called inside the room, "Thanks, Mr. Finlayson," pulled the door closed himself, and then pushed the cart in the direction that led away from the office toward the end of the long one-story motel building.

Moriarty relaxed again. Just the laundry. Usual thing. Dirty sheets in a laundry cart. He waited some more.

The boy and the laundry cart disappeared around the corner of the building. Moriarty returned his eyes to the front door of Room 116. Odd. The drapes were slightly apart. He hadn't noticed that before.

Just then there was a movement toward the end of

the building. It was the kid coming back. But he didn't have the laundry cart. Where was it?

Then Patsy Moriarty realized. Standard procedure at a motel was to pick up the laundry, but you didn't wheel the cart into the room. The cart stayed outside the door. This cart had gone into the room, so Finlayson could sneak out inside it, under a sheet.

"Goddamn it," Moriarty hissed and jumped from the car, not bothering to conceal his pistol.

He ran up to the youth, who was sauntering back toward the office, whistling.

"Where's the cart, kid?" he said, grabbing the youth by the shoulder.

The youth started to pull away, saw the pistol and froze. He pointed toward the end of the building. "I left it down there."

"And it had somebody in it," Moriarty said.

The youth looked blank.

Moriarty released his shoulder and began to run toward the end of the building. The youth ran in the other direction, toward the office.

Between the two of them, Dr. Harold Smith carefully opened the door of Room 116 and stuck his head out. He saw Moriarty turn the corner at the end of the building.

Smith ran to his tan Dodge, unlocked it, got in and started the engine. It caught quickly. He raced it once, slipped it into reverse, and backed out of his parking spot. Then he dropped it into low drive, and turned it toward the end of the building.

Moriarty, after turning the corner, saw the cart at the end of a long driveway where tall weeds seemed to encroach on motel property. A sheet lay on the ground next to the cart.

The man had run into the weeds to hide, Moriarty

realized. He kept running toward the cart. He'd track him down if it took forever.

Too late, he heard the whirring behind him.

He turned, gun in hand, but the tan Dodge was on him. And then he felt the pain as the front of the car, moving at high speed, slammed into his body, and he felt himself crumple, then he was lifted high in the air and it seemed as if somebody else's body was turning those lazy loops. The gun slipped from his hand, and then his body spiraled toward the ground twenty feet away. The last thing he felt was his head slamming against a heavy stone and the last thing he ever thought was to wonder if he had scored the night before or not, and then everything went black for Patsy Moriarty. Forever.

Smith, who had once commissioned a study on the effects of auto impact on human bodies, knew Moriarty was dead. He had seen the pistol drop from the man's dead hand and he got out of the car now and picked it up. It saved him one errand for the day.

Now he would casually drive away. He backed the car up, turned it around and drove slowly out the side entrance of the Happy Haven motel, whistling. It had been a long time since he had been operational, almost thirty years. It felt rather good.

He drove the car until he overtook a bus. He sped up, parked two blocks ahead, then got out and boarded the bus to wherever it went. He would buy another car, and then start making some telephone calls.

His day was just starting.

CHAPTER FIFTEEN

Services at the funeral home the night before had been a strain on Holly Broon. IDC personnel from all over the country, wanting to see and be seen, had shown up. And of course there had been the politicians, bankers, brokers, competitors, and the hustlers on the make. Accordingly, there had been a continuous stream of visitors to the small overwhelmed funeral home in the quiet Connecticut town, and Holly Broon had had to be hostess, bereaved daughter and confidante to all of them, and she was tired. So she slept late.

She was awakened by her personal maid who tiptoed to the side of her bed and waited silently until Holly Broon awakened just by sensing her presence.

The young woman opened her eyes, stretched, saw the maid and asked, "What is it?"

"I'm sorry, Miss Broon," the slender blonde girl said in a delicate British accent, "but there is a man on the phone who insists on talking with you."

"So? That's something unusual around here? Hang up on him."

The maid did not move.

"For Christ's sake, what is it, Jessie?"

"I'm sorry, Miss Broon, but he said he had something to tell you about your father, and that you would want to know it."

"Probably that daddy was a great guy."

"No, miss. He said it was about the way your father died."

Holly Broon sat up in bed. She had pretended her father's death had been nothing but a heart attack. So the call might mean something. "All right," she said, "I'll talk to him."

"Yes, miss. You're not angry with me?"

"No, Jessie. Go now. I'll take the call here."

Holly Broon waited until the blonde girl had left her room before stretching her left hand toward the telephone.

"Hello," she said.

"Hello," came a dry crisp voice. There were a lot of ways to say hello. Some people were questioning; some were unsure of themselves; some were brisk and abrupt, trying to cover indecisiveness with the all-business mask. But the greeting she had just heard was the hello of a man totally rational and in control of himself and everything that he dealt with.

"You don't know me," the voice went on, "but I have some information about the death of your father."

"Yes?"

"I noticed in the press that an attempt was made to make your father's death seem natural. But, of course, it wasn't. The death of your father was the work of Blake Corbish."

Holly Broon laughed. "I'm sorry, but that's ridiculous." She knew whom she was talking to now. "Corbish wouldn't have the nerve. It would take seven months of committee meetings for him to make such a decision."

"I don't mean, Miss Broon, that he performed the . . . er, matter himself. I mean he ordered it done."

"How do you know that?"

"Miss Broon, I know a number of things about Mr. Corbish. Is it not so that he is now in line to succeed your father as president of IDC? Wouldn't you think that was motive enough?"

Holly thought about that for a moment. "Yes, I guess it might. But if Corbish didn't do it himself, who did?"

The voice hesitated only momentarily. "No doubt he hired someone to do it. Please, Miss Broon, I am giving you this information so that you can act on it, and also so that you can protect yourself."

"I appreciate it," Holly Broon said, adding playfully, "You sure you won't tell me who you are?"

"It's not important. Do you know what Corbish is up to?"

"Yes, I think I do."

"It is very dangerous; he must be stopped."

"Do you really think so, Dr. Smith?"

Speaking his name brought a click to the other end of the connection. Holly Broon laughed.

It had probably been dumb, but she had not been able to resist. Yet the laughter stopped as abruptly as it started.

There was little doubt in her mind that Smith had told her the truth. She had begun to suspect it herself after that first day of watching Corbish in operation. He had ordered the killing of her father, presuming that he would immediately become the president of IDC. And she had played right into his hands.

Now she had a decision to make. Should she stop Corbish? Or should she go along and let him become president of IDC and then extract her revenge later? She thought about it for a moment, but her mind focused on a chilling question: could she stop Corbish? Did he have resources that she knew nothing about that might guarantee him the IDC presidency with or without her?

Even while wrestling with the question in her mind, Holly Broon knew the answer. She knew what she would do.

Blake Corbish would be stopped. Anyway she had to.

Outside a rural phone booth in Pennsylvania, Dr. Harold Smith felt vaguely dissatisfied.

He had broken the news to the Broon girl about Corbish's implication in her father's death. And she had guessed who he was. That meant she had at least an inkling of what Corbish was up to. She might even have been in on it from the start.

He doubted it.

It would be strange to find a woman who would cheerfully go along with the planning of her father's murder. She had probably wised up after the fact.

He hoped that she would put a little heat on Corbish. That would help.

But there was something else that was disquieting to Smith.

Holly Broon might not know much about what Corbish was doing, but she knew something.

And something was too much. She would have to die also.

It was a shame, he decided. She sounded like a bright woman.

CHAPTER SIXTEEN

"He's nuts, Chiun. Absolutely stark raving nuts."

Remo stood in their White Plains hotel room, the telephone in his hand, staring at the instrument as if he would find an answer there to the eternal riddle of man's inhumanity to man.

"You refer to your Mr. Garbage?"

"Yeah," said Remo, deciding that correcting Chiun's pronunciation was no longer worthwhile. "I just called him. You know what I got?"

"A headache," Chiun suggested. "Another reason for your interminable kvetching?" Without waiting for an answer, he looked down again at the parchment on which he had been writing.

Remo decided to be magnanimous and ignore that. "I got a switchboard, for God's sake. Can you picture that? A switchboard. The dopey bastard wants me to talk to him over an open line."

Remo was outraged. Chiun was mildly amused when he looked up. "It is a difficult thing, is it not, this serving

139

of a new and strange Emperor. When you grow up, you may learn that."

"Anyway, he's going to call me back here on a private line."

"I am happy for you, Remo." Chiun did not seem happy.

Remo put the telephone down. "Why do you say that?"

"I mean, it is best for you to take your little victories as they come. Having Mr. Garbage call you back. That is wonderful. Not having to wear your silly little plastic badge when you go to see him. That is wonderful. At least you should think those things are wonderful, because Mr. Garbage is going to make sure that nothing else in your life is wonderful."

"Meaning?"

"Meaning that you are an assassin who has been given the secrets of Sinanju. But Mr. Garbage does not recognize that this makes you something special, or would if you were a more worthy student. No. To him you are just another person with a pencil and one of those funny yellow writing tablets with blue lines. He sends you out to go looking for people, when looking for people is not what you should do. He will someday, if he sees you are not busy, start asking you to empty wastepaper baskets. He is a fool. And you are a bigger fool for serving him. Thank heaven that I have almost completed my history of Dr. Smith and his insanity. At least, in history, the House of Sinanju will not be regarded as a part of this foolishness."

The telephone rang and Remo yanked it to his ear.

"I want you to come and see me. In my office," came Corbish's voice. "And who authorized you to move out of the sanitarium?"

"I did," Remo said. "I decided it was stupid for me to hang around there. I was too visible."

"Before you do anything like that again," Corbish said, "you'd better check it with me."

"Whatever you want."

"Be here in half an hour," Corbish said.

Remo snarled and hung up the telephone.

"Don't forget to wear your little plastic badge," Chiun said.

When he reached Folcroft, Remo went over the stone wall, up the wall of the building and through a window into Corbish's office.

Corbish was not alone. Sitting across from him was the bosomy brown-haired girl Remo had seen that night in Broon's house. She was wearing what Remo regarded as a ridiculously wasteful black dress which almost but not quite hid her body, but should nevertheless have been blamed for even trying.

Remo was through the window, heading for the floor when he saw Corbish's guest. He curled his legs up before he hit, twisted his body, and landed softly, using the long curve of his right leg as a rocker. He rolled quietly to his feet.

Corbish saw the movement and looked up. The girl saw nothing, heard nothing, but spotted the surprise on Corbish's face and followed his gaze. Remo stood there in front of the open window, looking at both of them, feeling stupid.

"Hi, folks," he said. "Can I get you something from the bar? Scotch? Vodka? A Spritzer made with Snow White?"

"Who is this lunatic?" asked Holly Broon, turning back to Corbish.

"It's all right, Holly. He works for us." He stood and walked toward Remo. "Really, fella," he said. "The office door would have been perfectly adequate."

"I keep forgetting," Remo said.

141

"Holly, this is Remo. Remo, this is Miss Broon. You read about her father's recent death, I take it?"

It was very subtle, except that it did not fool Holly Broon who knew, as soon as she heard Corbish, that Remo was the man who had killed her father.

"Yup, I read about it," Remo said. "Sorry, Miss Broon."

"Kindly omit flowers," she said.

"Uh, yes," said Corbish. "Come outside, Remo, I have to talk to you a moment."

He took Remo's elbow and led him into a small room off Smith's main office. The room was decorated with a plastic-topped desk and two metal folding chairs. Corbish closed the door tightly behind them.

"You've got to take care of Smith. Now," he said.

"Why?"

"He killed a man today."

"Oh? Who?"

Corbish cleared his throat. "Somebody tracked him down outside Pittsburgh. Smith ran him over with a car."

"Who was this somebody?"

"Does it matter?"

"Yes," Remo said.

"He was, I guess, you'd call him a hoodlum."

"And why was a hoodlum going after Smith?" Remo's tone was indignant.

"Well, if you have to know, although I can't see why any of this concerns you, I put some people on his trail."

"That's swell," Remo said in disgust. "That's just swell. I really need that, right? I really need people cluttering things up? I'll tell you, Corbish. Smith would never have done it this way."

"What would he have done?" Corbish seemed really interested.

"He would have told me who the target was. If he knew, he would tell me *where* he was. And then he

142

would get the hell out of the way and let me do my job."

"That's what I'm doing now," Corbish said. "Remo, go do your job."

"Arf, arf," said Remo. "Do you know where Smith is?"

"No."

"Corbish, let me tell you something. You're not going to last here."

Corbish smiled a thin-lipped smile. "I may outlive you."

"Maybe. But just maybe," Remo said. "But you're definitely going to outlive anybody who gets in my way. I don't want a gang of goons trailing Smith all around the country."

"I just thought they might be able to find him faster than you could."

"You leave that to me. No interference," Remo said.

"Whatever you want," Corbish agreed. "Can you do the job? No emotional attachments?"

"I do what I have to do," Remo said.

"Good. You're my kind of man," Corbish said. Remo shuddered. Corbish opened a side door from the small office. "This leads to the outside corridor. If you're shy about seeing the office staff, you can go through here. Do you have your badge for the gate?"

"Got it right here," said Remo, patting his empty shirt pocket.

"Good fella. Put it on and the guards won't bother you."

"That's nice. I'd hate for the guards to bother me."

Remo started toward the door. Corbish bent down to pick up a piece of newspaper from the floor. He tossed it to Remo. "There's a trash can outside. Dump this in it, will you?"

Remo took the paper. "Sure thing, *bwana*. Can this boy go now?"

"Keep in touch."

He closed the door behind Remo who began to shred the old newspaper into confetti. Chiun was right. This dizzo would have him emptying wastepaper baskets before long. Remo's hands moved like high-speed knives across the surface of the newspapers. Chips and strips of paper fluttered through the air until the last shred was gone from Remo's hands. The hall looked as if it had been the scene of a confetti convention. So much for recycling.

Remo went down the stairs, out into the bright sunlight and headed straight for the wall. The hell with the gate, the guards and Corbish. The hell with everything.

Corbish returned to his desk.

"Sorry for the interruption, Holly. Now what was it?"

"Who is he?" Holly Broon asked.

"Just a hired hand. He goes with the place," said Corbish, trying a smile on for size.

"Does he always come through a window?"

"He's rather eccentric. We're not going to have him around for too long."

No, Holly thought, just until he finishes any more killings you have lying around. All she said was, "I think that's a good idea. He looks unstable to me and he acts unbalanced. What'd you say his name was?"

"Remo. But I'm sure you didn't come here to talk about him."

"No, I didn't, as a matter of fact. I came to talk about the board of directors meeting. I think it should be postponed."

Corbish's face dropped open. "Postponed? Why?"

"Well, my father's being buried tomorrow. I've given it some thought and it would seem like rushing it a little to elect a new president the next day. I think we ought to wait a little while."

"But . . ."

"Oh, I don't mean for long. Just two weeks or so," she said.

Corbish picked up the old straight pen on his desk. He began to twirl it between the fingertips of both hands, as if it were a piece of clay he was trying to soften.

He looked at Holly, who was smiling at him, blandly and openly.

"Well, if you think it's best," he said. "What do the board members say?"

"I haven't spoken to them about this," she said. "But they'll follow my lead in the matter. You know them. A pack of jellyfish."

Corbish nodded. "Well, as you say. Let's fix a date, though, for the meeting."

"No hurry," Holly Broon said. She stood up abruptly. "We'll do it after the funeral."

"Bye now," she added brightly, turned and walked away from the almost president of IDC, whose gloom hung like a heavy drape over his face.

"Well, that's it, Chiun," said Remo. "I've been told to get Smith."

"What will you do?" Chiun asked.

"What would Smith do if he had the assignment?"

"If he were sane, he would go after you."

"Well?"

Chiun broke into a burst of Korean expletives, then hissed at Remo in English: "But he is only an emperor and they have never been honored for their sense or wisdom. However, you are a student of Sinanju and should know better. You are even more than that. You

145

are almost a member of the House. Turning on your emperor is unthinkable."

"Chiun, you just don't understand. Smith isn't my emperor. My emperor is the government, and right now, Corbish is giving orders for the government."

"Then let us all pity this government of yours. Go! Go kill Smith."

"I didn't say that."

"Tell me whenever it is you say what you are going to say." Chiun turned away in disgust.

"All right. This is what I want to say. I've been given an assignment. Eliminate Smith. So I'm going to eliminate Smith. That's it. Case closed."

"Where will you find him?"

"I don't know."

"Do not worry about it."

"No?"

"No," insisted Chiun. "Smith will let you know where he is."

"How do you know that?"

"Because he is only a madman, but you are a fool. And I am the Master of Sinanju."

And then Chiun would say no more, but returned to writing on his heavy parchment with the goose quill pen.

At the moment, Smith was the problem furthest from Blake Corbish's mind.

Holly Broon's announcement that she would not call the executive board meeting had shocked him. And he wondered if she had learned or guessed that he had somehow been involved in her father's death. If she had, she might be trying to block his appointment for good, and if that were the case, he had problems. He needed her name and support to get the presidency of IDC.

Unless . . .

Corbish fiddled with the pen on his desk for a while, then grabbed a pencil and began to work out a computer program. For the first time since Remo had left, he thought of Smith and he hoped that Smith and his CURE computer system were as thorough as he believed they were.

They were.

An hour later, rolling out in printouts under the glass panel on Corbish's desk were reports on the nine old men who made up IDC's executive board.

He smiled when he saw the first one. He broke into a grin on the second, and on the third he was hissing under his breath to himself. By the ninth he was laughing aloud, almost uncontrollably.

A string of facts and evidence. Tax-dodging, illegal corporate structures, daughters with abortions, sons with criminal records, wives with habits like shoplifting. Smith's computers had noted everything.

Corbish let out a gleeful whoop. With the information the computer had just given him, he could guarantee, absolutely guarantee, the votes of every man on the executive board.

So much for Holly Broon. Let her think she had stopped him. When the executive board did meet, it would be Blake Corbish who would be chosen. She had been a fool to think she could put him down so easily, as if he were someone who was careless.

Corbish ripped off the computer printouts sheets and put them in his top desk drawer. No need to leave them around; no time to be careless.

But Blake Corbish had already been careless.

He had failed to notice that each man written up on the printouts had had an item added as of that day. This would have been hard to determine, because the

147

date of the information was in a string of code numbers at the end of each individual item. One had to look carefully for the date to find it.

There was a simple explanation for the late items. They had been put there that very day by Dr. Harold W. Smith.

After talking to Holly Broon, Smith had realized that Corbish's first move would be to take over IDC. If Holly Broon believed Smith about the death of her father, she would try to stop Corbish and he would have to go after the executive board to get the job.

From a thick blue book in a public library, Smith had gotten the names of the executive board members. Then, armed with his change maker, he had gone to a row of telephone booths in a sleepy shopping center and begun to make phone calls.

One went to a newspaperman in Des Moines. Another went to a police captain in Jersey City. Another went to the plant manager of a federal installation outside Philadelphia and another to a postal inspector in California. Call after call, across the country, to different types of people in different walks of life, all joined by one common denominator: without knowing it, they worked for CURE.

They were all professional gossips, and for their gossip they often received cash stipends. They were all part of Smith's informal but effective nationwide information-gathering system.

Except in this case there was a difference. The information Smith gave them, under the guise of being an anonymous tipster, was false. Smith had dreamed up a string of lies about the nine men on the IDC board. He did not know what steps Corbish might take, but if he had the sense to use CURE's information against the men, Smith had decided to complicate the process by putting in some false information. Perhaps Corbish might overplay his hand.

Those phone calls took a big part of Smith's day. When he was done, there was one more piece of business to perform. He put a dime into the telephone, dialed the number and waited for the operator to cut in. "That will be $1.60 for three minutes," she said.

"Right here, operator," said Smith, clicking off six quarters and using the initial dime which she had returned.

He was running low on quarters and would have to restock, he noted idly.

"Thank you," the operator said.

"You're welcome."

A moment later, Smith heard the buzz of a ringing phone. It rang for twenty seconds before it was picked up by a female voice.

"Hello?"

"Hello, dear, this is Harold."

"Harold, where have you been?"

"Away on business, dear," Smith said. "But I'm all right. How are you?"

"I'm fine, dear. And so is Vickie. When are you coming home?"

"Soon, dear. Very soon. Listen dear, this is important. Do you have a pencil?"

"Yes. Right here."

"All right. A man will call on you, seeking information about me. When he comes, tell him this. He should go to Washington, D.C., and rent a room in the Lafayette Hotel under the name of J. Walker. I will contact him there. Do you have that?"

"I think so. Washington, D.C. Lafayette Hotel. Room in name of J. Walker. You'll contact him."

"Very good, dear."

"By the way, Harold. What is the name of this man who'll be calling?"

"His name is Remo."

"Why, Harold, what a funny name."

CHAPTER SEVENTEEN

"Is this Remo?" asked the woman's voice.

"Yes. Who are you?"

"This is Holly Broon. We met today in Corbish's office?"

"Sure," said Remo. "Where'd you get my number?"

"I called the switchboard at Folcroft. They told me where to find you."

"Oh, good," said Remo. "That's swell. For a minute there, I thought somebody might be giving my number out indiscriminately. But as long as the switchboard is only giving it out to everyone who calls, well that's okay."

"I'd like to see you tonight. Could I?"

"Sure. Time and place?"

"My house. Forty minutes. I'm in Darien," she said, and gave him an address and directions.

"I'll be there," said Remo. He turned to Chiun.

"Do you know how she got our phone number?" he asked.

"Mr. Garbage advertised it in the small print in one

of your newspapers?" suggested Chiun, without looking up from the parchment on which he was still writing.

"No, but he might just as well have."

"Give him time. He will. If you live that long."

"Or if he does," Remo said. "I've got to go out for a while."

"Go," said Chiun. "I am reaching a critical point in my history of the mad emperor Smith."

When Remo drove his rented car up in front of the Broon estate in Darien, a butler was waiting at the front door.

"Mr. Remo?" he said.

Remo nodded.

"Right this way sir," the butler said.

It was great, Remo thought, being a celebrity. Another two weeks of working for Corbish and everyone in the country would know him. His face would be more famous than Howard Cosell's; his name more well known than Johnny Carson's; and Remo himself would be more dead than Kealey's nuts.

The butler led him up a broad center stairway to a second-floor suite of rooms. He pushed open the door, stepped aside, let Remo enter and closed the door behind him.

Remo went in, looked around, and realized with some amusement that it might just be the first living room he had entered by invitation in ten years. He had gotten used to skulking in through a window or forcing a door. But Remo was there as a guest, not as a killer stalking someone. It was an eerie feeling, rejoining the human race.

He sat back in a chair, savoring the moment, waiting for Holly Broon. How nice to be in a living room, waiting for someone who expected you, secure in the knowledge that when that person greeted you it would not be with gun in hand.

A door to a connecting room opened and Holly Broon, tall and full-figured in a violet silk wrap, stood there. She held a gun in her hand.

Remo noticed it, but noticed even more the long line of thigh which jutted out from the opening of her wrap. It was doubly sensuous in the heavy shadows cast by the old-fashioned lighting in the room.

"Mr. Remo," she said.

Remo stood. "You always greet your guests this way?"

"Only the ones I'm going to kill."

"Kill me with kindness. It's my weak spot."

"The only one?"

Remo nodded.

Holly Broon pushed the door shut behind her and came into the room. She was a woman, and experience had made Remo cautious of women with guns.

With men there was a logical sequence of steps, an intensity that mounted steadily, until at the flash point of emotion they pulled the trigger. A carefully tuned-in man could read that sequence and act at just the right time. But with women it was different. They could pull the trigger at any moment, because their minds and emotions didn't follow any normal sequence of steps. They might fire because they thought it was going to rain, or because they thought it wasn't going to rain. They might shoot because they remembered the grease spot on the green tulle dress in the closet. Anything might do it, so Remo would watch her. He would act as if the gun wasn't in her hand. He would keep her calm at any cost. That was the safest thing to do.

Holly Broon screamed, "You son of a bitch," and squeezed the trigger. Remo saw the telltale tensing of her knuckles just before her finger squeezed the trigger.

153

Without bracing himself, and from a full stand, he flipped his body backwards over a large chair, landing on his neck and shoulders on the soft carpet behind the chair. The room was filled with the crack of the bullet from Holly Broon's pistol. Behind him, Remo heard the window crack as the bullet shattered the glass and went out into the rich Connecticut hills, where it would no doubt be stopped by nothing more important than a peasant.

"Son of a bitch," Holly screamed again. "Why'd you kill my father?"

Remo heard her feet pounding across the rug toward him. She would, of course, be holding the gun in front of her. He moved to his feet. When she reached him, she squeezed her right index finger again. Nothing happened. The gun was no longer there. Instead it was between Remo's fingers, plucked from her hand so fast she had not seen his hand move.

Remo examined the gun as if it were a particularly interesting bug, then he tossed it over his shoulder. He put an arm around the woman's shoulders. "There, there," he said. "Tell me all about it." He would calm her down until he could find out how she had learned about him.

Holly Broon balled her fist and punched him in the stomach.

"Ooooph," Remo grunted. She wrenched loose from his protective arm and went diving across the floor for the revolver, her satin robe hiking its way up around her lush thighs as she did. Her hand was near the revolver when Remo landed on the floor beside her.

He slapped the gun away, this time under a large mahogany chest.

"Now, now," he said. "What's this all about?"

She sobbed in his arms on the floor. "You killed my father."

"Who told you that?"

"Doctor Smith."

"When'd you talk to him?"

"This morning. He called me. Is it true?"

"Now do I look like the killer type?"

"Then Corbish did it, right?"

Remo nodded, and then because he felt terrible about lying to the poor girl, he made love to her. As he did, he wondered why Smith had called. He really was demented, trying to cause trouble for the new head of CURE that way. Compromising Remo in the bargain. The more he thought of it, the more angry he became. When Remo saw him, he would give him a piece of his mind, he thought. Then he remembered with a chill that when he saw him, he would have to kill him. That took all the fun out of pleasuring Holly Broon—although she did not seem to be able to tell the difference. She moved and moaned beneath him, even though he had trouble concentrating.

"Oh, Remo," she said. "I'm so glad it wasn't you."

"Me, too," he said, since he could think of nothing else to say.

He left her with her eyes closed on the plush carpet of her drawing room, a peaceful look on her face, a smile on her lips. He stood up, arranged his clothes, and looked down at her naked body. Women should always look so happy, he thought. There would be much less violence in the world.

He turned and walked toward the door. Let her rest. If she wanted to settle the score with Corbish later on, let her. That was Corbish's problem. And hers. But not Remo's. Thank God, he was out of this one.

As he reached the door and extended his hand toward the knob, the click of a pistol's hammer alerted his senses. He collapsed onto the floor. Right where his head had been, a bullet slammed into the door, ripping out a large chunk of the heavy oak. Remo pushed open the door and rolled through the opening.

In the hall, he was on his feet and running.

Nuts, he thought.

Everybody in the whole world was nuts.

He would hold this view for at least another thirty minutes, while he was driving back to his hotel and saw a large sign reading Folcroft Oaks Golf Course. The sign triggered a memory and Remo recalled that Smith told him once he lived on the edge of a fairway. Yes, he remembered, Smith had a family. A wife and a daughter, just like real people. Just like Remo would never have. And if anyone knew where Smith was, Mrs. Smith would.

Driving along the golf course road, Remo suddenly understood the telegram Smith had sent him. "When are you going to hit a home run?"

It meant Remo should look for Smith at his home. He had been tantalizing Remo all along. But why?

Remo drove the darkened deserted grounds of the golf course until he saw an old English tudor house with a small sign in front of it: *Smith.*

Under normal circumstances, he would have sneaked into the house. But a taste for going in front doors had been reawakened in him. He parked his car in the driveway, walked to the front door and rang the bell.

A chubby middle-aged woman in a light blue knee-length dress answered the bell on the third ring.

"I'm looking for Dr. Smith," Remo said. "Is he in?"

"Your name is?"

"My name is Remo."

"Oh, yes, I've been expecting you. Harold called and left a message for you. Now, let's see, what was it? Oh, yes. He said you should go to Washington and rent a

156

room in the Lafayette Hotel under the name of J. Walker and he would contact you there."

"Did he say when I should do this?" asked Remo.

"Oh, my goodness, no. He didn't say. But he sounded as if it was important, so I would guess he meant right away."

"I see," Remo said. "Thank you."

"Are you sure you have it right, Mr. Remo? I'll write it down if you want."

"No, that's all right, Mrs. Smith. I'll remember it."

He started to walk away, but stopped when Smith's wife called:

"Mr. Remo?"

"Yes?"

"Is my Harold all right? He's not in any trouble, is he?"

"Not that I know of."

"Good," she said and her face brightened. "He was sort of abrupt on the phone. Do you work with him, Mr. Remo?"

"I used to."

"Well, I feel better about that, because you're a very nice young man. Would you like to come in for a cup of coffee?"

"No. I'd better be going," Remo said.

"When you see Harold, give him my love," the woman said to Remo's retreating back. He turned and looked at her, framed in the doorway, and for a moment he felt jealous of old penny-pinching Smith and ashamed of himself for what he would have to do when he found him.

157

CHAPTER EIGHTEEN

"It is done," Chiun said.

Remo looked blankly toward Chiun and shrugged his shoulders.

"I said, it is done."

Remo shrugged again. Aboard the American Airlines jet to Washington, Chiun reached over and plucked from Remo's ears the stethoscope-type earphones on which Remo was listening to a stereo music concert.

"What, Little Father?" said Remo, rubbing his ears.

"Nothing," Chiun said.

"It must have been something for you to tear my ears off."

"It was unimportant."

"Okay. Call me when we get to Washington," said Remo. He lowered his body in the seat and closed his eyes as if to sleep.

Chiun stared at Remo's closed eyes. "You will sleep a long time," he hissed, "before the Master of Sinanju speaks to you again."

Remo opened his eyes. "What's the matter, Chiun?"

"My history of the Smith dynasty is complete. Yet, do you care? Even though you are in it? Do you care to learn how history will regard you? No. You want to listen to be-bops and to sleep."

"Nobody listens to be-bops anymore," Remo said.

"If anyone could, you would."

"Let me see your history."

"I don't know if I should," Chiun said.

"Then don't," said Remo.

"Since you insist," Chiun said, and he held out the long roll of parchment on which he had written.

Remo sat up straight, took the scroll, unrolled it from the top and began to read. Chiun's handwriting was big and elaborate, decorated with swirls and loops, like a Palmer Penman gone berserk.

Chiun's Mad Emperor

In the middle part of the twentieth Western century, there was in a land across the big water, an emperor named Smith. He was also called Doctor Smith, as if this should be a title of respect, but few knew him and even fewer respected him.

It was to this land, then called the United States of America, that the Master came those many years ago, and in the service of the Emperor Smith did find himself.

But there was no wisdom in this Emperor Smith and he did not deal with the Master in truth and friendship, but made the Master instead responsible for trying to train baboons to play violins. Still, the Master worked with dignity and honor and loyalty for years for Smith, doing all that was asked of him, and doing it without words of anger, spite, or unceasing complaint. (This was unusual in that land at that time, because the native people were much given to complaining of things which, was called kvetching. But this was not a surprise to the Master, since they were a people without culture and, in fact, produced nothing of value to the world except dignified stories of troubled people, which they showed to the Master on a special picture box that was then called television.) The Master remained in the service of Smith because it was an evil time in Sinanju and it was necessary that gold be sent to care for the poor and the sick and the young and the old.

Among the many services the Master performed with honor for Emperor Smith was the training of a man as the Master's assistant, which is a kind of servant. To this man, the Master gave some of the secrets of Sinanju, but he did not give all of them because this servant was incapable of grasping them, but the Master did give him enough to teach him to come in out of the rain. This made the servant a man unique in that day and age in the land called the United States.

Smith was not a truly evil emperor since he fulfilled his bargain with the Master and always provided the tribute due to the village of Sinanju, and it was right that he should do this.

But toward the end of his reign, Smith began to lose his senses. The Master, of course, in his wisdom saw this but he did not confide it to anyone since in a land where no one has all his wits about him, Smith might have gone on for many years, a stark, raving lunatic, but apparently normal and still emperor.

However, in quiet ways, the Master tried to help Smith by offering him advice on how to stay in power and how not to be overthrown by his enemies. But Smith would not heed.

Then, one day, while the Master was away from Smith's palace on a most important mission, Smith disappeared. There will be those who might say that this was the Master's fault; that some blame should be placed upon him for this.

But let all who read these words heed these facts and reject this complaint as untruth. The Master worried about Smith, but if Smith waited until the Master was away on a mission and took that precise moment to go fully insane and to wander out into the vast uncharted wildernesses of his country, then the Master could not be blamed.

Is this not so?

A word about the kind of emperor Smith was. While he was the emperor and himself paid the tribute to the Master of Sinanju, he was chosen as emperor by another man, who was a type of overlord chosen by all the people of that country in a national disgrace called an election.

And this overlord chose as the new emperor a man whose mind was even more unstrung than Smith's.

And this new emperor, whose name was that of Garbage, wanted the Master to do many things, most of them demeaning and all of them stupid. The Master would not do these things. Instead, he allowed his servant whose name was Remo, and who was unable to tell a crazed mind from a healthy one, to do those things.

And that servant was called upon to destroy the mad emperor Smith, and many things happened before the matter was resolved to everyone's satisfaction.

However, it was agreed by everyone, and even the overlord who was above the emperor, that the Master of Sinanju had covered himself again with glory and honor, even though in the service of a madman, and it was agreed by all the people of this land called the United States of America, that the Master was a man of wisdom and justice, and could not be blamed for what a crazed emperor might try to do when the Master was many thousands of miles away in a place they called at that time Grosse Pointe.

All hail the Master of Sinanju.

Remo finished reading and rolled up the scroll again. "Well?" Chiun demanded.

"I'd give it a pretty good mark."

"What is it, this pretty good mark?"

"I'd give you an A for style and originality of thought, but only a C minus for content, and a D for penmanship."

"Is that all good?" asked Chiun.

"Yes," said Remo. "It's very good."

"I am pleased," Chiun said, "because it is important that the world know the entire truth about this unfortunate incident of Smith's madness."

"No worry about that anymore," Remo said. "Not now that you've got all the straight dope down on paper."

"Parchment. I have written it for the ages."

"You have done wonderfully," Remo said.

"Thank you, Remo. It is most important."

And then both were silent until they had left the plane, taxied to Washington and checked into the Lafayette Hotel under the name of J. Walker and Mr. Park.

Remo had convinced Chiun that they would not stay in Washington for the night. He had thereby persuaded Chiun that he did not need to bring his usual seven trunks of robe changes. Instead, Chiun carried only a silken scarf which was filled with things that he insisted were necessary for his well-being, including his written record of the perfidy of Smith.

Remo turned on the television set and he and Chiun sat on the floor to wait, but before the set had even warmed up, the telephone rang.

Remo went to the phone.

The voice that spoke to him was Smith's. For a moment, Remo felt almost pleased to hear the lemon-sour humorless whine again and to realize that Smith was alive. That feeling lasted only until Smith had completed his first sentence.

"Trust you to ignore the air shuttle and catch a first-class flight to Washington."

"What have you done?" Remo asked. "Gone into the travel agency business?"

"Not yet," Smith said. "Are you here to kill me?"

"Those are my orders."

"Do you believe I'm insane?"

"I always believed you were insane."

"All right. We might as well get on with it. In an hour, I'll be in Room 224 of the Windsor Park Hotel. That's just off Pennsylvania Avenue. It's now 9:36. I'll see you there at 10:35."

"Okay, Smitty."

All Remo heard was a click in his ear. It was annoying. He had wanted to tell Smith that his wife had been asking for him.

Remo turned to Chiun. "Smith," he explained.

Chiun rose slowly, his dark brown robe swirling about his sandaled feet.

"And now?"

"I'm going to meet him."

"And?"

"And do what you trained me to do."

Chiun shook his head. "You should not," he said. "You have a contract with Smith. Who is this Mr. Garbage that he should order you to violate that contract?"

163

"He is my new boss. My emperor."

"Then he is emperor of a kingdom of fools. I am going with you."

"I don't want you to, Chiun," said Remo.

"I know you do not and that is why I am going. To protect you from your stupidity. Some day you will set down your own history and I want you to be able to set it down with truth and honesty, as I did, so that men will know you did what was best. If I do not go with you, you will do what is stupid."

"How do you know that?"

"Because it is what you do best."

CHAPTER NINETEEN

The door to Room 224 of the Windsor Park Hotel was
unlocked.

Remo pushed it open and stepped inside. He might
have had contempt for Smith as a skinflint, but he never
figured him for a fool, so he moved in carefully, alert,
ready to move if Smith had somehow booby-trapped him.

Chiun followed Remo into the darkened room. Remo
looked around and at the far right of the room, he could
see a man sitting in a chair.

"Close the door," came Smith's voice. "The light is
on the left-hand wall."

Instinctively, from ten years of habit, Remo obeyed.
He closed the door first and then turned on the light.
Two lamps on the dresser went on, illuminating the room.

Remo turned, looked at Smith and laughed. Smith
was sitting in a chair at the far-right corner of the room,
next to a radiator. There were handcuffs on his wrists
and the cuffs passed under one of the heat riser pipes
of the radiator, so that Smith could not move unless his
hands were freed. Then Remo noticed something else.

There was a heavy cord in Smith's hands. It looped up to the far wall, where it passed through a screw-eye. The cord moved through a series of screw-eyes along the top of the wall, and then stopped at some kind of device over the door. The device was complicated looking, but it was simple enough for Remo to see that it included two sticks of dynamite.

A damned bomb. Remo turned back to Smith, a complimentary smile on his face.

"Nice going, Smitty," he said. "What makes you think that pile of junk will work?" he asked, nodding over his shoulder toward the bomb over the door.

"Hello, Chiun," Smith said. To Remo, he said, "Explosives were one of my specialties in the war. World War II. It'll work."

"What's the point?" asked Remo. "You know I could shoot you before you pull that string."

"If you carried a gun. But I know a few things about you, Remo. One is that you never carry a weapon."

"I can get you with my hands."

"True," Smith said. "And as I fall, the weight of my body'll set off the bomb."

Remo nodded. "True enough. Stalemate. Now what?"

"I wanted to talk to you with a guarantee that you wouldn't do anything foolish or impulsive."

"Like kill you?"

"Exactly," Smith said. "Sit down on the couch, please."

Remo moved across the room to sit on the sofa. Chiun still stood near the door, looking up at the dynamite.

"Now what I wanted to talk about was this," Smith said. "Corbish is a fraud. He's a vice president of IDC who drugged me and took over CURE's operation. Without authority, without orders, without the right. Remo, he's dangerous. He could bring this country down."

"He told me you'd probably say something like that,"

Remo said. "What about the letter turning authority over to him?"

"I wrote that letter ten years ago, Remo. He tortured it out of me."

"He said you'd say that too."

"Do I sound to you as if I'm insane?"

"You and Corbish both sound insane. So now what?"

"There is one man who can tell you the truth," Smith said. "I haven't been able to reach him."

Remo nodded, knowing the man Smith meant.

"But you could reach him," Smith said. "And he could tell you the truth."

Remo nodded again.

"So what I want you to do," Smith said, "is go see him. Ask him. And then when he tells you I'm still in charge, we'll go and get Corbish the hell out of there before he destroys the country."

Remo looked at Chiun, who was nodding. He was being taken in by this, he thought. Time to set him right.

"Knock it off, Smitty," Remo said. "You know damned well that as soon as we leave, you'll be heading out the door."

"That's idiotic, even by your standards," Smith said. "Do you really think I arranged to meet you in Washington so that I could try to escape from you? Arrant nonsense. But I thought you might think that. On the arm of the couch there"—he nodded with his head—"are the keys to these handcuffs. I can't escape unless you unlock them. Go. Find out. I'll be here when you come back."

"That is good sense, Remo," said Chiun. "He will be here when you get back. And then you will have peace of mind in what you do, because conflicting orders are bad for the soul."

"And if I say no?" Remo asked Smith.

"Then CURE is gone and with it, maybe the country,"

said Smith. "And I don't want to live in a country like that anymore. So I won't. And neither will you," he said, raising his hands with the bomb pull cord between them.

Remo got to his feet and dropped the handcuff key into his shirt pocket. "All right, Smitty. This time I'll do it. I'll go ask him. But watch out if this is a wild goose chase."

"It isn't, Remo. Just go."

Remo moved toward the door. "All right, all right, we're going."

He stopped in the doorway and turned back toward Smith.

"By the way, your wife sends her love."

"Thank you," Smith said.

Holly Broon, after firing her last desperate shot at Remo from a small Derringer she had kept concealed in her satin dressing gown, got to her feet.

She did not believe Remo at all. That he had killed her father she did not doubt, but neither did she doubt that the killing had been ordered by Blake Corbish.

Her body felt tired, languid, with the afterglow of lovemaking, but the pleasurable sensations quickly gave way to the frustration she felt at having missed Remo with the shot.

She retrieved her police special from under the mahogany cabinet, walked into her bedroom and went to the telephone stand. She dialed a number and fell back on the bed while the phone rang.

"Oh, hello, Mrs. Corbish. May I speak with your husband, please? Yes, just tell him this is Holly." Holly Broon could not resist the implied intimacy of the first-name identification. As she waited for Corbish, she thought again of Remo. He was a rare one, a fighter *and* a lover. It was an interesting combination. Perhaps he might yet be salvageable. A big corporation like IDC could use a man like that. And for that matter, why restrict it to IDC? The country could use a man like him, particularly if, as she hoped, one day Holly Broon would run the country.

"Oh, yes, Blake, how are you? Fine. Blake, I've been thinking and perhaps we might have that board of directors meeting on schedule the day after tomorrow. But I'd like to talk to you about it. Yes, tonight. Suppose you drive over and pick me up? I'll be ready. We can drive somewhere and talk. Yes. Forty-five minutes will be fine."

She picked a brown two-piece suit out of the closet. It was uncharacteristically modest, but it had the major virtue of having deep wide pockets which could discreetly contain a gun.

Corbish hung up the phone and noted that oddly his feelings were mixed. He should have been overjoyed but he wasn't. He pondered a moment, then realized what was wrong: he had looked forward to the chance to break down the nine members of the IDC executive board with the information he had gotten on them from CURE's files. It would have been fun, to pick them apart, one at a time, a secret at a time, until they were nothing but piles of bones at Corbish's feet.

But Corbish had learned to take victory as it came. It had come now in the person of Holly Broon. Let it go at that.

"So it's Holly, is it?" Corbish was jolted back to reality by his wife's abrasive voice. His wife was standing behind him, ever-present martini glass in her hand.

"Yes, it's Holly. Holly Broon. She owns IDC."

"It sounded like she thinks she owns you too."

"She does, Teri. She owns everything and everybody

in IDC. And soon I'm going to share the ownership of it with her."

"Will there be any left for me?" she demanded.

He pushed roughly past her. "Sure there will. Enough to keep you in gin and vermouth. Have another. Have another dozen," he said.

Forty-five minutes later, Corbish was pulling into the driveway of the Broon estate. He started to park the car but Holly Broon came walking down the front stairs, wearing a dark suit and carrying a large handbag. He was glad now that he had worn a sports jacket and slacks.

"Hello, Blake," she said, entering the car.

"Hello, Holly. Anyplace special you'd like to go?"

"Drive for a while. Better yet, go north. We've got a camp on the edge of the Sound. We could stop there."

It took twenty-five minutes to get to the camp which was a camp in name only. It was a multi-roomed mansion of redwood, glass and fieldstone, and in the glare of Corbish's headlights, the stones crackled with imbedded pieces of glass, making the base of the house appear as if it had been inlaid with diamonds.

His whole world would soon be inlaid with diamonds, Corbish thought. First IDC and then the country. And then? Well, who could ever tell? He must dare to dare greatly. Who had said that? Bobby Kennedy? Teddy Roosevelt? It didn't matter. He would say it someday, and make it his own.

Holly Broon had slipped out of the car and was walking around the front through the headlights. Corbish turned off the engine and the lights and got out onto the hard-packed gravel.

"Before we go in, let's go down to the shore," she said.

"Sure."

"It's beautiful this time of year."

Corbish grunted agreement. He cared little or nothing

about beauty and would have sworn that Holly Broon, in that regard, was a kindred spirit. So what was it? A seduction attempt again? Perhaps, but he hoped not. He didn't really care for that sort of thing.

He followed her down a long string of stone steps that ended abruptly at the water's edge. The grass grew down almost to the rocks. Metal chairs dotted the grass, and spike-tipped drink holders stuck into the grass wavered eerily in the slight breeze, reflecting the moon's rays like so many chrome arrows.

Corbish put his hand out idly and touched one of the drink holders, setting it vibrating from side to side. Holly Broon's back was to him as she looked out at the Sound. Softly, she began to talk.

"I spoke to your man, Remo, tonight," she said. "He told me that you ordered my father killed."

"Remo said . . ." Corbish was suddenly alert.

"No, don't interrupt," she said. "He said you ordered my father's death. Dr. Smith told me the same thing this morning. I just wanted you to know that I know."

Corbish was stunned. So she had learned. Was she going to take it smoothly? Perhaps she had wanted the old man dead as much as Corbish did. She must have. He felt almost relaxed. She continued to talk on, softly, and Corbish pulled one of the drink-holders out of the soft sod, and felt its sharp spiked end.

"I know you wanted him killed because you thought he would stand in the way of your getting power. I just want you to know that I understand." Her voice rose just slightly in pitch and Corbish came to attention again. He saw her hand go toward her pocket. "I understand," she repeated. "It's the same reason I'm going to kill you. Because you stand in the way of my getting power."

The hand was out of the pocket now, holding the revolver, and Holly Broon whirled to fire.

171

She squeezed the trigger. But Corbish had dropped into a squatting position and the bullet whizzed by his head. Then Corbish sprang forward, holding the drink-holder in front of him like a sword. He planted its point in Holly Broon's abdomen and let the force of his body press it through, skewering her like a Wasp-ka-bob.

She screamed once, a loud piercing scream, and dropped her pistol. Blake got to his feet, withdrew the drink holder and then stabbed her again with it, in the chest. This time, he released it, and the woman dropped heavily to the ground at his feet.

"You bastard," she hissed. Water from the Sound trickled into her mouth and she coughed. Her hair, whitish in the bright moonlight, floated idly around her face like loose spiderwebs drifting in a breeze, her eyes opened wide, then her head dropped to her side.

Corbish looked down at the dead body. What's done is done, he thought. He realized that Remo would have to die too because he was the last one who knew about Corbish's role in the Broon death.

Corbish spent a half hour at the scene, cleaning and replacing the murder weapon, assuring himself there were no prints left on it. He dragged the woman's body to a small nearby cove with a heavy overhang of branches, tied an anchor to it, and wedged it into a small crevice underwater, between two rocks. There would be time for him to come back and dispose of it properly later.

Then Corbish went back up the stairs toward his car. He decided to go to Folcroft and begin working on the list of the nine board members of IDC. He would need to assure their votes now that Holly Broon could not speak out for or against him.

He whistled as he started his car and began to back

out of the long driveway. Two down. Broon and his daughter. Two more to go. Smith and Remo.

Smith waited until he was sure Remo and Chiun had gone, then pulled the cord leading to the bomb. It disengaged itself from the wall behind the dynamite where Smith had stuck it with tape, and fell harmlessly to the floor. Smith smiled to himself as he reached onto the window sill for the spare key to the handcuffs, unlocked them and freed himself.

Good, he thought. Remo had fallen for it. If he got through to the one man who could clear up the question of CURE's leadership, there would be nothing to worry about. But if Remo could not, when he returned, he would find Smith gone. And Remo would be out of Smith's way when Smith returned to Folcroft, where he had business to take care of: Blake Corbish.

Before leaving, he wrote a note for Remo.

"Have returned to Folcroft. Don't worry about the dynamite. It's fake. —H.S."

CHAPTER TWENTY

The most important resident of 1600 Pennsylvania Avenue was jolted from his sleep by a hand pressed over his mouth.

A voice close to his ear in the darkened bedroom hissed, "Don't shout and I'll let you go. You're in no danger."

The man in bed nodded and felt the hand move away from his mouth. He turned toward the other bed in the room. In the black silence, he heard the rhythmic slurps of air from his wife.

He turned again to the night visitor.

"I have a question to ask," the visitor said.

"What network are you with?"

"No network, sir. Just one question."

"You know I can have this place crawling with Secret Service men in twenty seconds."

"Don't count on those four outside in the hall. They're napping. Now, the question. I know all about the secret agency, CURE. I know that Dr. Smith was running it for you. My question is, did you remove him and appoint a new man?"

The man in the bed hesitated. CURE was the country's deepest secret. No one had dropped a loose word about it in more than ten years. He vowed not to be the first.

"CURE?" he said. "I know nothing of any CURE."

"Please," came the voice, again close to his ear. "I work for CURE. I have to know who's running it. It's for the good of the country."

The man in the bed paused. The voice hissed again: "Is Dr. Smith still the head of CURE?"

The man hesitated, then said softly, "Yes."

"Thank you," came the voice. "We'll leave you now. It was nice seeing you again."

The man in the bed remembered. Over a year ago, someone had accosted him in the hallway and whispered a children's song to him. Was this that person? The enforcement arm of CURE?

The man in bed heard the stranger move away from him. He hissed into the darkness, "Are you that special person?"

"Yes, I am. Good night, Mr. President."

And then the President of the United States saw the door open and the figure of a man move out; behind him he saw a wizened, wispily bearded old man, who seemed to be dressed in an Oriental robe. The President thought this was very curious; the door closed, and the more he thought about it, the more he realized he was dreaming and he finally closed his eyes and went back to sleep, hoping he could recapture his previous dream in which he had been a court constable, serving warrants on newspapermen who failed to pay their bar bills.

Remo and Chiun moved through the darkened White House, then out a window to a second-floor balcony.

Noiselessly, they slid down the side of the building and moved back toward the iron fence. They scaled it, landing softly on the sidewalk, and began walking away from the main entrance to the building.

"He is a very nice man," Chiun said.

"If you like the type."

"I will never again believe what those vile correspondents of television say about him."

"Well, I never believed much of that anyway."

"Why do they have those vile correspondents on television? Why do they not have more of those beautiful dramas?" Chiun asked.

"I guess they figure people couldn't stand so much beauty."

In the darkness, Chiun nodded his head. "That is probably true. Beauty is hard for most people to deal with."

"Step it up, Chiun," said Remo. "We've got to go back and release Smith."

"Are you not glad you did not kill him?"

"Yes, I am. Tell you the truth, I prefer him to Corbish. He's gonna be sore as hell we took so long to get back."

"Smith will not be angry," Chiun said.

"Why?"

"He is not there."

Remo snorted.

"He's not here, Chiun."

"Of course not."

"The dynamite was a fake."

"Of course. Why else would it bear the legend on the bottom: Hong Kong Fireworks Company?"

"He's gone back to Folcroft."

"Of course. That is where we must go."

176

Smith drove the short distance from Kennedy Airport to Folcroft with uncharacteristic speed. He had just made his plane to New York. Remo and Chiun would be following him soon. They might even be landing now.

No matter. He had time.

Up ahead, he saw the faint glimmer that indicated the lights were on in his office behind the one-way glass. He slowed and drove past the main gate of Folcroft. That was something new. Uniformed guards were on duty. It would be foolhardy to try to get past them.

He drove past the Folcroft grounds and three quarters of a mile down the road, where he made a sharp left turn onto a dirt road. The road wound its way down a long incline until it stopped at the water's edge in the midst of a string of vacation cabins. Smith turned off his lights and engine and got out of the car. After a moment, his eyes became used to the dark and he saw what he wanted, a small rowboat, with an electric trolling motor, tied up to a dock.

Smith smiled slightly to himself. It was almost like wartime again. In those days, they called the theft of property "a moonlight requisition." Well, this really was a moonlight requisition.

He clambered into the rowboat and using one oar as a paddle, moved it slowly away from the dock. He waited until he was thirty yards out into the Sound before starting the electric trolling motor which caught with a faint whir. Then he moved to the seat at the back of the boat and turned its nose north towards Folcroft.

CHAPTER TWENTY-ONE

Blake Corbish fished the printouts on the nine executive board members of IDC from his top desk drawer, arranged them carefully on his desk, and began to read again.

But his mind, he found, wasn't on it. Nor was it on the body of Holly Broon, now buried beside Long Island Sound.

No, he found his mind wandering to the telephone on his desk. Where was Remo? Why hadn't he called with a report on Smith? He tried to fix his eyes on the printouts, but unconsciously they drifted away from the paper and back to the telephone. Why the hell didn't Remo call? After all the switchboard was now open twenty-four hours a day; Remo would have no trouble getting through. Call, dammit, call.

Corbish spun in his chair and looked at the one-way windows. The lights in the room bounced off the glass and he was annoyed that he could not see the Sound, only a brief glimmer occasionally that must have been a light from a passing boat.

How many times had Smith sat here just like this, waiting for the telephone to ring? And he had done it for how many years? Ten years? Of waiting for phone calls, waiting for reports? For a moment, he felt almost a tinge of sympathy for Smith. He had probably done a fine job. His setup of the computer operation was nothing short of brilliant; and how well he handled the pressure of the job was proved by his longevity in it. Ten years. It could be an eternity in a job such as director of CURE.

It was just rather a shame that Smith had gotten old. But it happened to everyone, just another way station on the road to death. Smith was probably well along that road now, Corbish thought. But he'd still feel better when Remo called.

Smith, however, did not consider himself on the road to death. Actually, he was walking a path between rows of shiny stainless steel pots and pans in the basement kitchen of Folcroft, heading for an elevator that led upstairs to the main office complex.

"Doctor Smith!" came a heavily accented woman's voice. "When did you get back?"

Smith turned. The woman was a short, buxom matron, wearing a blue uniform and a broad smile.

"Hello, Hildie," Smith said. "I just returned." He kept walking toward the elevator.

"Did you enjoy your vacation?" she asked.

So that was the cover story. Smith was pleased; it would adequately explain his sudden reappearance.

"Very nice, Hildie," he said. "I saw the country."

"Well, I am glad you are back. I do not mind to tell you that this Mr. Corbish—Oh, all right, I guess he is a very smart man and all, but he is not you, Doctor Smith."

Suddenly, Smith felt hungry.

"Hildie, is there any yogurt? Prune whip?"

"No one eats it since you left and Corbish"—gone

179

already was the Mister—"says don't buy it, cause it'll just be wasting." She smiled even more broadly. "But I bought some anyway. I hid it in the back of the big icebox."

"Good girl, Hildie," said Smith, considering and then rejecting the idea of docking her salary the cost of the yogurt since she had bought it despite instructions. "Would you put some on lettuce for me?"

"Bring it to the office, should I?"

"Yes."

"Right away," the woman said.

"No," Smith said quickly. "Not right away." He looked at his watch for a moment, then said: "In seventeen minutes."

"You got it, Doctor Smith," she said, looking at her own wristwatch. "Should we symphonize our watches? Like they do in the spy movies?"

Smith smiled his thin-lipped grimace. "No, Hildie. We'd get it all wrong. What do we know about spy movies?"

He turned and continued walking toward the elevator.

The door to Smith's office had always squeaked. Blake Corbish had found this terribly annoying, and one of his first acts had been to have a maintenance man oil the hinges. When that didn't totally silence the door, he had had the hinges replaced.

The door was now absolutely silent. Without warning, Blake Corbish heard a voice behind him say, "Hello, Corbish."

Corbish wheeled in his chair, shocked. Shock turned to horror when he saw Smith.

For a moment, he could not get words out of his mouth. Then he said, "How . . . Smith . . . how . . . ?"

"How isn't really important now, is it?" Smith said

180

coldly. "I'm here. That really should be more than enough for you to worry about, by itself."

Corbish moved to his feet; Smith's hand moved to his pocket and brought out a .45 caliber automatic.

"Well, well," Corbish said. "A weapon. I wouldn't have suspected it of you."

"I don't generally carry them," Smith said. "But this was a gift. From a man who tried to kill me in a Pittsburgh motel."

Smith waved the gun at Corbish. "Sit back down. You've got time yet. There are some things I want to know."

"You think I'll tell you?"

"Yes, I think so," Smith said, his eyes locked with Corbish's, the words coming from his mouth even though his lips did not even seem to move. "It's rather interesting, but we once had a study done here. It showed that forty-eight hours was the absolute limit that a man could withstand torture. I know you'll talk."

Corbish grimaced. He knew the study. Smith had proved that it was accurate. "What do you want to know?"

He expected Smith to quiz him on changes in procedure, in personnel, in the operation of the computers. Instead, Smith asked, "What have you carried outside this building?"

"Excuse me?"

"Have you taken any papers home?"

"No," Corbish said, answering truthfully.

"All right. Who else knows what this place is? Besides Broon, that is. He took his information with him."

"No one."

"Not even his daughter?" Smith said. His tone of voice made it clear he knew Corbish was lying. Corbish could

181

see Smith's hand tighten around the grip of the automatic.

"I wasn't thinking of her," Corbish said. "She's dead."

"You?"

Corbish nodded, and picked up the straight pen from his desk, twirling it nervously between his fingers.

"Well, then I guess we have everything we need, don't we?" said Smith.

"How did you get away from Remo?" Corbish asked.

"When I left him, he was verifying just who was supposed to run this organization. By now, I'm sure he knows you are an impostor."

Corbish grinned. He dropped the pen and stood up. "It wouldn't matter, you know, what anyone else told him. Give me five minutes with him, and I'd have him believing the moon is made of cheese."

Another voice came from the doorway.

"The only cheese in this place is you." It was Remo's voice.

Smith turned slightly toward the door, just enough to see Remo and Chiun in the open doorway, and just enough to enable Corbish to reach across the desk and pull the automatic out of Smith's hand.

"All right, you two," he called, waving the automatic. "Move in here. Close the door."

Chiun closed the door. He and Remo moved toward the front of the room. Smith stood motionless at the side of the desk.

"I told you once before," Corbish said to Smith, a savage smile on his mouth, "you're too old for this sort of thing. Now we're going to have to retire you. All three of you. With honors, of course."

"Just an academic question," Smith said. "Were you telling me the truth? You took nothing out of here?"

"Yes, it was the truth. Why would I need to take anything out? I've got everything I need right here. Everything."

Smith nodded.

Chiun moved slightly away from Remo, as Remo kept moving toward the window side of the room. Corbish followed both of them with his eyes, first one, then the other.

When there was five feet between them, Corbish yelled, "All right, you two, stop right there."

"Mr. Garbage," called Chiun.

Corbish looked to the old Oriental. As soon as his eyes moved, Smith reached down and snatched the straight pen up from Corbish's desk. Turning it over in his hand, he swung his right arm forward, and the pen, point-first, smashed into Corbish's right eye. Smith pressed until the point and the pen stopped.

Corbish's mouth dropped open. The pen stuck from his right eye socket like some hideously misplaced antenna on a Martian mutant. A sound started to come from his mouth. The gun dropped from his hand and thudded on the desk.

"I . . . I . . ." he said, then fell forward onto the desk. As he fell, the end of the pen slammed against the desk blotter and the weight of his falling body drove it deeper, through his eye and into his brain.

He paused on the edge of the desk there for a moment, as if frozen, and then his body slowly slid off and dropped to the floor.

"Not enough wrist action," Remo said.

Smith turned to him.

"No," Remo said, "I'm not kidding. When you do something like that you've got to snap the wrist at the last moment. Almost like cracking a whip. That's what gives the extra zip."

Smith looked at Chiun.

183

"Is this what I pay you to teach him?" he said. He pronounced "him" as if it were an obscenity.

"He is not much of a pupil," Chiun said. "But he is improving. For instance, he always knew you were not mad. Just as I did," he added hastily. "We are happy you have returned so that we can get on with our business."

"Oh?" Remo said. "*We* always knew he wasn't mad? Is that right? Is that right? Show him the parchment, Chiun. Show him the history you wrote."

Chiun shot an evil look at Remo. "The good doctor would not be interested. Besides it was only a first draft; it requires revisions yet."

"As soon as it's done, Smitty," said Remo. "As soon as it's done, I'll Xerox it and send you a copy."

"I would prefer it," said Smith, "if you would just get rid of this garbage." He motioned to Corbish's body. "Take it with you when you go. And go immediately. I thought you were under firm orders never to come here."

"Well, actually . . ."

"Never mind actually. Just leave," Smith said.

Remo came behind the desk and hoisted Corbish onto his shoulder. He fell in behind Chiun, heading for the door.

In the doorway, he stopped and turned back to Smith.

"Go," Smith said.

"I can't, said Remo.

"Why not?"

"The guards won't let me pass. I forgot my plastic name tag."

Meet MALKO: SPYMASTER

Prince Malko is the spy of the seventies! He's one of the CIA's most daring and effective "special agents." That means he gets the impossible missions, the dirty jobs.

This series is being made into major films in the James Bond tradition. Harold Robbins, bestselling author says of Malko (France's #1 bestselling series): "Tremendous tales of high adventure and espionage." Read the books— *before* you see the movies.

MALKO by Gerard de Villiers

ORDER HERE:

To: Pinnacle Books, 275 Madison Avenue, New York, N.Y. 10016
Please send me the titles I have checked above. Enclosed is my check or money order for the cover price of the book(s) . . . plus 25¢ per book for postage up to 4 books (thereafter free).

Name_____

Address_____

City_____State_____Zip_____
_____Check here if you wish to receive our free catalog.

PB-27

THE INCREDIBLE ACTION PACKED SERIES

DEATH
MERCHANT

by Joseph Rosenberger

His name is Richard Camellion, he's a master of disguise, deception and destruction. He does what the CIA and FBI cannot do.

Order		Title	Book #	Price
	# 1	THE DEATH MERCHANT	P211	$ .95
	# 2	OPERATION OVERKILL	P245	$ .95
	# 3	THE PSYCHOTRON PLOT	P117	$ .95
	# 4	CHINESE CONSPIRACY	P168	$ .95
	# 5	SATAN STRIKE	P182	$ .95
	# 6	ALBANIAN CONNECTION	P670	$1.25
	# 7	CASTRO FILE	P264	$ .95
	# 8	BILLIONAIRE MISSION	P339	$ .95
	# 9	THE LASER WAR	P399	$ .95
	#10	THE MAINLINE PLOT	P473	$1.25
	#11	MANHATTAN WIPEOUT	P561	$1.25
	#12	THE KGB FRAME	P642	$1.25
	#13	THE MATO GROSSO HORROR	P705	$1.25
	#14	VENGEANCE OF THE GOLDEN HAWK	P796	$1.25
	#15	THE IRON SWASTIKA PLOT	P823	$1.25
	#16	INVASION OF THE CLONES	P857	$1.25
	#17	THE ZEMLYA EXPEDITION	P880	$1.25

TO ORDER

Please check the space next to the book/s you want, send this order form together with your check or money order, include the price of the book/s and 25¢ for handling and mailing to:
PINNACLE BOOKS, INC. / P.O. BOX 4347
Grand Central Station / New York, N.Y. 10017

☐ CHECK HERE IF YOU WANT A FREE CATALOG

I have enclosed $_____check_____or money order_____as payment in full. No C.O.D.'s.

Name_____

Address_____

City_____State_____Zip_____
(Please allow time for delivery.)   PB-36

THE PENETRATOR

by Lionel Derrick

Mark Hardin. Discharged from the army, after service in Vietnam. His military career was over. But *his* war was just beginning. His reason for living and reason for dying become the same—to stamp out crime and corruption wherever he finds it. He is deadly; he is unpredictable; and he is dedicated. He is The Penetrator!

Read all of him in:

Order		Title	Book No.	Price
_____	# 1	THE TARGET IS H	P236	$ .95
_____	# 2	BLOOD ON THE STRIP	P237	$ .95
_____	# 3	CAPITOL HELL	P318	$ .95
_____	# 4	HIJACKING MANHATTAN	P338	$ .95
_____	# 5	MARDI GRAS MASSACRE	P378	$ .95
_____	# 6	TOKYO PURPLE	P434	$1.25
_____	# 7	BAJA BANDIDOS	P502	$1.25
_____	# 8	THE NORTHWEST CONTRACT	P540	$1.25
_____	# 9	DODGE CITY BOMBERS	P627	$1.25
_____	#10	THE HELLBOMB FLIGHT	P690	$1.25

THE RAZONI & JACKSON SERIES

One's black, one's white—they're young and the ballsiest detectives on the city beat! Dynamite—and exclusively from Pinnacle!

by W. B. MURPHY

THE "BUTCHER,"
the only man to leave
the Mafia—and live!
A man forever on the run,
unable to trust anyone,
condemned to a life
of constant violence!

THE BUTCHER SERIES

Order		Title	Book #	Price
_____	# 1	KILL QUICK OR DIE	P011	.95
_____	# 2	COME WATCH HIM DIE	P025	.95
_____	# 3	KEEPERS OF DEATH	P603	1.25
_____	# 4	BLOOD DEBT	P111	.95
_____	# 5	DEADLY DEAL	P152	.95
_____	# 6	KILL TIME	P197	.95
_____	# 7	DEATH RACE	P228	.95
_____	# 8	FIRE BOMB	P608	1.25
_____	# 9	SEALED WITH BLOOD	P279	.95
_____	#10	THE DEADLY DOCTOR	P291	.95
_____	#11	VALLEY OF DEATH	P332	.95
_____	#12	KILLER'S CARGO	P429	1.25
_____	#13	BLOOD VENGEANCE	P539	1.25
_____	#14	AFRICAN CONTRACT	P583	1.25
_____	#15	KILL GENTLY, BUT SURE	P671	1.25
_____	#16	SUICIDE IN SAN JUAN	P726	1.25
_____	#17	THE CUBANO CAPER	P794	1.25
_____	#18	THE U.N. AFFAIR	P843	1.25
_____	#19	MAYDAY OVER MANHATTAN	P869	1.25
_____	#20	THE HOLLYWOOD ASSASSIN	P893	1.25

TO ORDER
Please check the space next to the book/s you want, send this order form
together with your check or money order, include the price of the book/s
and 25¢ for handling and mailing to:
PINNACLE BOOKS, INC. / P.O. BOX 4347
Grand Central Station / New York, N.Y. 10017
☐ CHECK HERE IF YOU WANT A FREE CATALOG
I have enclosed $_____check_____or money order_____as
payment in full. No C.O.D.'s

Name_____

Address_____

City_____State_____Zip_____
(Please allow time for delivery.)   PB-37